BLOOD BOND
SHOOTOUT AT GOLD CREEK

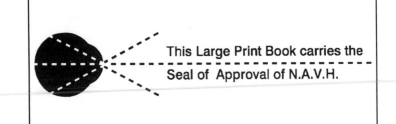

This Large Print Book carries the
Seal of Approval of N.A.V.H.

BLOOD BOND SHOOTOUT AT GOLD CREEK

WILLIAM W. JOHNSTONE

THORNDIKE PRESS

An imprint of Thomson Gale, a part of The Thomson Corporation

Detroit • New York • San Francisco • New Haven, Conn. • Waterville, Maine • London

THOMSON
★
GALE

LIBRARY OF CONGRESS CATALOGING-IN-PUBLICATION DATA

Johnstone, William W.
  Blood bond. Shootout at Gold Creek / by William W. Johnstone.
    p. cm. — (Thorndike Press large print western)
  ISBN-13: 978-0-7862-9751-1 (alk. paper)
  ISBN-10: 0-7862-9751-4 (alk. paper)
  >1. Gold miners — Rocky Mountains — Fiction. 2. Colorado — Fiction.
3. Large type books. I. Title. II. Title: Shootout at Gold Creek.
PS3560.O415B558 2007
813'.54—dc22   2007017967

Published in 2007 by arrangement with Pinnacle Books,
an imprint of Kensington Publishing Corp.

Printed in the United States of America on permanent paper
10 9 8 7 6 5 4 3 2 1

BLOOD BOND
SHOOTOUT AT GOLD CREEK

CHAPTER ONE

"We've got trouble, Boss."

Clarence Hart looked up from the machinery he was working on, his tanned skin glistening in the light of the setting sun. Touches of gray were sprinkled through his brown hair and laugh lines had started to form around his mouth. Though he was no longer a young man, years of hard work had made his muscles rock-hard and he was as strong as most men half his age. In this rough-and-tumble mining community composed almost exclusively of men, he worked shirtless. His shoulder muscles rippled as he stretched, trying to work out the kinks that working in a tight spot had given him.

The young man standing before him repeated his statement. "We've got trouble. It's Jordan's bunch. They're moving in on Shannahan down at the creek."

Hart clenched and unclenched his fists. His blue eyes, usually twinkling with good humor, now seemed almost a flat gray. He looked at the broken-down mining machinery that still needed repair. He had hoped to have the repairs completed before dark. No matter. The safety of his men was more important than any machine.

"How many?"

"Only a few, but the ringleader is one of the new hands that Jordan brought in. The one that wears the fancy holster tied low."

Hart mentally reviewed the new faces in the area. There were many who could be considered hired guns, brought in by Nelson Jordan. His enemy's move had left Hart no choice but to bring in some guns of his own. Hart had strength and courage. He had years of working in and around mines that had sharpened his mind and forged his muscles into bands of iron. He could also shoot as well as most Western men, but against a professional gunfighter he wouldn't stand a chance, just as his men wouldn't stand a chance. This particular gunfighter would be the one they called Parrish. He wasn't one of the best guns in the West, but he was still dangerous. And unfortunately, Hart did not have the kind of money it took to hire guns that were as fast and dangerous as the ones that Jordan had hired. At this point, it was still Hart and his men against Jordan and his hired guns.

The young messenger, Tom Tyler, was barely more than a kid. He was an honest, hard worker. Shannahan, an Irishman just a few years older than Tom, was a former boxer from the old country who had come to the new world to seek his fortune. His other men were of the same type. In a fair fight, they could hold their own. But would they stand a chance against the men that Jordan was bringing in?

Hart continued to clench and unclench his massive fists as Tom watched anxiously. Hart knew that every second he hesitated could bring Shannahan that much closer to death. Jordan had done everything he could that was even close to legal to take over Hart's claims and meager mining operations. Now Jordan was raising the stakes with the gunfighters. It wouldn't be beyond him to kill Hart's men in cold blood, if that was what it would take to make Hart sign over his deeds.

Hart also knew that if he stood up to Parrish he might also be a dead man.

No matter. He hadn't mined and prospected for most of his life, finally finding the best vein he had ever seen, only to lose it to the likes of Nelson Jordan! Hart would die before letting that happen.

9

The older miner stood, reached for a well-used Winchester.

"Are you with me, Tom?"

"I'll follow you into the pits of hell itself," the younger man answered. "We all would. You know that."

"That just may be where we're headed," Hart answered grimly. "But if so, we'll go down fighting like hell!"

The sun setting beyond the dark hills cast coppery shadows on the two men riding leisurely down the well-rutted trail. In the distance, sounds of mining machinery could be heard and the burning odors from the smelter crowded out the natural smells of pine and night air.

"I'm not sure I like the smell of this town," Sam August Webster Two-Wolves said, laughing slightly. "I've smelled trouble before, but never an aroma quite like this!"

"I've seen some privies that smelled sweeter," Matt Bodine agreed, holding his nose with an exaggerated motion.

"Still, where there's mining, there's sure to be someplace for a beer. We've been riding long enough. I could handle the stink for a cool beer and a good card game."

"Ever the philosopher, Sam?" Matt said.

"I didn't spend those years in college for

nothing!" Sam answered.

Both men laughed and continued their good-natured kidding. Though they rode leisurely, as if they hadn't a care in the world, each man kept his gun hand free. And their eyes constantly scanned the areas on each side of the trail, their ears listening for any sound that might hint of danger. They had been through many adventures and survived countless fights because of the caution that had become second nature to them and the easy way they worked together. They had learned from experience to always be prepared for any kind of trouble that might jump out at them from the next bend in the road.

The closeness of the two men came as natural as breathing for in truth they were blood brothers.

In the reddish shadows, the two men looked quite similar, as might be expected from brothers. Each was young, handsome, and muscular, over six feet tall and weighing over 200 pounds. They were dressed simply, in comfortable clothes covered with trail dust. Around their necks each man wore identical multi-colored stones pierced by rawhide in the Indian style. On a first, casual glance, they could pass for full brothers, and had many times.

A closer inspection, however, revealed a number of differences. Though both had a wild and reckless glint in their eyes, Matt had blue eyes and brown hair and Sam had black eyes and black hair. Sam's other features, however, had been inherited from his white mother. Only his cold obsidian eyes, which were occasionally softened with high humor, gave away his Indian heritage.

In spite of the different cultures they represented, the two young men were as much blood brothers as if they had the same mother and father. They were joined by knife and fire and the Cheyenne blood-bond ritual brought them closer together than most white men could ever conceive or know.

Sam's father had been a great and highly respected chief of the Cheyenne, his mother a beautiful and highly educated white woman from the East who had fallen in love with the handsome Cheyenne chief and married him in Christian and Indian ceremonies. As boys, Matt had saved Sam's life. Though his home was on a nearby ranch, Matt had spent as much time in the Cheyenne camp when he was growing up as at his home on the ranch. He was finally adopted into the Cheyenne tribe, thus becoming a True Human Being according to Cheyenne beliefs.

Sam's father, Medicine Horse, had been killed during the Battle of the Little Big Horn after he charged Custer, alone, unarmed except for a coup stick. When Sam's father realized that war was coming and that he must fight, he ordered Sam from the Indian encampment and to adopt the white man's ways and to forever forget his Cheyenne blood.

Matt and Sam had witnessed the subsequent slaughter at the Little Big Horn, though that was a secret only they shared. In the sad time that followed the battle, they decided to drift for a time across the rugged West to try and erase the terrible memory of the battle.

Though they looked like drifters, in truth they were well-educated and wealthy. Sam Two-Wolves was college educated, while Matt had been educated at home by his mother, a trained schoolteacher. Sam's mother had come from a rich Eastern family and left him with many resources, which Sam had used to his advantage. Matt had earned his fortune through hard work and smart business moves. He had worked riding shotgun for gold shipments and as an Army Scout, saved his money, and bought land. Both Matt and Sam now owned profitable cattle and horse ranches along the Wyoming-Montana border.

The two men never looked for trouble, but neither did they ever back away from a fight, which caused them to be involved in many adventures.

And through their exploits, the two blood brothers were developing an unsought but well-deserved reputation as gunfighters.

As Matt and Sam continued to ride, they came upon the outskirts of the community itself. Dozens of tents had been erected, with a few ramshackle wooden buildings thrown in to break the monotony. At one point in the rutted road, a rough wooden sign had been nailed to a post. Toward the bottom of the sign were the words "Silver Creek." It had been crossed out and a new name painted in: "Jordanville."

Sam pointed to the sign and suggested, "Seems the people of this town can't make up its mind about what to call themselves."

"It's not much of a town now," Matt answered. "Probably isn't even organized yet. You know how these new mining towns are. They pop up one day, and gone the next. I saw lots of these towns when I was riding shotgun."

Now Sam's keen senses picked up the smell of the river among the unpleasant

14

odors of too many humans in too small of a space and the fumes from the mining operations.

The sound of the bullwhip was less subtle.

It cracked, and cracked again, piercing through the night.

The two brothers looked at each other.

"What do you think?" Matt asked. "Should we keep riding? It's not our problem."

"You know how I feel about whips," Sam said.

"Probably the only law here is by the gun. If we ride on in and take a look, we'll probably get ourselves involved in another fight."

Sam continued as if he hadn't heard his brother. His eyes had grown hard as he thought about injustices he had seen in his life. He said, "No beast or man should ever be subjected to that kind of shame . . . or pain."

"Oh, hell," Matt answered.

"You know how I feel," Sam said. "I just can't ride by and let any man or beast be bullwhipped."

"Yeah, I knew you were going to say that. There goes any chance for a quiet beer."

Even so, Matt smiled slightly to himself, for he felt the same way that Sam did.

Without another word, both men spurred

their horses to greater speed toward the river, where the nasty sound of the bullwhip had come from.

Chapter Two

As Matt and Sam rounded the corner, there was still plenty of light to judge the situation. On the bank was a tall man dressed in a broad, black hat. He wore two heavy revolvers in tied-down holsters and was holding a large bullwhip made of shiny black leather. The end was tinged in red from where it had torn flesh.

Just a few feet into the river, next to a long sluice used to separate gold from worthless rock, stood another man. He was tall and slim. He held no weapon except a shovel. He had been working without a shirt. Several small red welts oozed blood where the tip of the bullwhip had hit.

The man with the whip laughed. "Well, Shannahan, have you had enough yet to make you return to the old country? We don't need the likes of you or your boss here. If you take off now, I might let you live."

The man in the water said nothing.

The man in black waved his whip and laughed. "On the other hand, there's too many damned Irishmen in Ireland, as well. Might as well kill you now and be done with it."

On the riverbank stood many other men. Some of them wore guns and, like Parrish, had the appearance of hired guns. They laughed along with Parrish. Others wore plain clothes and had the look of simpler workers. Some of these moved restlessly from one foot to another, as if they wanted to help but could not. The majority seemed indifferent.

Shannahan finally crossed his arms against his chest, one hand still holding his shovel, and said plainly, "Parrish, you're a damnable coward."

Faster than the strike of a rattlesnake, Parrish flicked his wrist and the bullwhip cracked again. The Irishman tried to use his shovel as a shield, without success. Another red welt appeared, this one on his cheek. The man didn't flinch, however, even as the drop of red started to run down his cheek.

"I'd think twice about calling me names, son," Parrish replied, grinning broadly. "If I were you, I'd consider myself lucky that I'm just using the whip on you. If I really didn't like you, I would've already had a bullet through you. Probably several bullets."

The two blood brothers were still several hundred feet from the scene, but could clearly see and hear the exchange as they rode.

Matt sighed, and said, "It's none of our business, you know. For all we know, that man in the river could have stolen the other man's wife. Or worse, he could have stolen a horse."

"You know better than that, brother," Sam said, through clenched teeth. "We've both seen this scene too many times. You know what's going on as well as I do. And even if he did steal a woman, not even that crime is bad enough to be bullwhipped. Too many of my people have suffered that kind of fate. I don't plan to let anybody be bullwhipped if I can help it."

"Then I'm with you."

The two men had worked together long enough that only a few words were needed to develop a plan and put it into action.

"I'm going after Parrish," Sam said. "You just make sure the others stay clear."

Shannahan briefly touched the blood trickling down his cheek, glanced at it, then turned his attention back to his tormentor.

"I speak only the truth," Shannanan said.

"You're a damnable coward. Come out here and face me like a real man, and I'd prove to everybody here that you're not a man. Truth is, you know you'd stand no chance against me. You act brave up there when you have the gun and whip and I have only a shovel. I'm calling you like I see it. You're nothing but a low-down, razor-backed cur of a mongrel bitch. I suspect that your owner, Jordan, is probably your bastard father . . ."

Matt had to admire the way Shannahan was conducting himself. Though he knew he could be shot or crippled at any moment, he still stood his ground and tried to anger Parrish enough to make a mistake. It was a desperate gamble, one that looked like Shannahan would lose.

Blood had flushed the face of the gun-fighter. Parrish angrily raised his hand to crack the whip with full force across the other man when unexpectedly he heard a horse racing toward him through the crowd. The spectators ran and jumped out of the way. Parrish looked up in time to see a grim face with dark eyes that were as cold as obsidian bearing down on him. Before Parrish could react, the other man reached out and plucked the bullwhip from his hand. In one fluid motion he threw the whip into the river and dismounted his horse.

"Stranger, I don't know who you are, but you're a dead man."

"My name's Sam Two-Wolves, and I think I disagree with your assessment of the situation."

Sam's cool words, more appropriate to a drawing room discussion than to a potential shootout, made Parrish pause for another half-second. It was enough time for Sam to cross the remaining several feet and connect with a solid right to the jaw. Parrish landed on his rear on the edge of the river. He was not hurt, except in his pride. He angrily jumped up to face the stranger.

Parrish waited for several more seconds. Still nothing, except for some low grumbles.

The seconds seemed like hours before Parrish took a quick glance to his left.

Another man that looked as if he could be a brother to Sam Two-Wolves was nonchalantly leaning against a tree, his revolver held lazily in his hand, while the other men were carefully placing their weapons in a pile in front of them. A few of them looked to Parrish and shrugged. Others in the crowd were smiling.

"You're on your own now, Parrish," Matt said.

"Let's see what kind of stuff you're really

made of," Sam said. "Prove you're not a coward who needs a bullwhip to try to pretend he's a man."

Parrish turned back to face Sam. The gunfighter and Sam were about evenly matched in height and weight, but Parrish had his back to the wall. All eyes were watching him. He was the one challenged, and could not easily slip out of this fight.

"Well?" Sam continued. "What kind of man are you?"

Parrish suddenly took three steps and dived at Sam, driving his shoulder into the other man's belly. The gunfighter had tele-graphed his move, however, and Sam had prepared himself by bracing his feet on the ground and tensing his muscles. To Parrish it felt like he was hitting a brick wall. Sam brought down a clenched fist on the back of the other man's neck.

The man in black staggered and dropped to his knees. As he fell, he reached out and grabbed Sam's legs and pulled. Sam was caught off balance, but managed to fall backwards, away from the river. As he hit the ground, he kicked upwards. The toe of his well-worn but polished boot caught Par-rish on the chin, snapping his head back-wards.

The gunfighter, though dazed, caught

himself and jumped back to his feet. He tried to stomp at Sam's groin. Sam moved, caught most of the force in his side, forcing him to gasp slightly. Parrish dived and tried to pin Sam. They rolled on the riverbank and both came up swinging. Parrish's fists moved rapidly, but each blow was blocked by Sam, who responded with a similar attack.

Though the two men seemed to be fairly evenly matched, Sam was in better shape. Parrish tired first. He let his guard down slightly and it was the only opening Sam needed. He took a quick step inside of Parrish's swings and with a quick uppercut slammed his rock-hard fist into the gunfighter's chin. The crack of bone sounded loudly across the crowd and Parrish's eyes grew glassy.

Still, Parrish tried to come after him one more time. He was now quite slow and could not dodge Sam's final blow to the face.

The gunfighter started to slump to the ground. Sam caught him by his short collar, lifted him and walked into the river toward Shannahan, who was watching the spectacle in wide-eyed amazement. Sam picked up the whip, now floating lazily on the surface of the river.

"My brother and I apologize for interfering in your business, but I have this thing about whips," Sam said in an apologetic tone. "Hope you took no offense."

"None taken," Shannahan said.

"Then that's settled," Matt said from the river-bank. "Let's go get a beer!"

"Good idea," Sam agreed, dropping the gunfighter with a splash into the river, throwing the whip in after him.

As Sam and his new Irish friend waded back onto the riverbank, a small crowd of newcomers came into sight over a hill. In the lead was a large man. He was wearing no shirt and had specks of gray in his hair. Even in the fading light, his eyes shone with a fierce determination. Following him were several other men with similar expressions on their faces. A few carried guns. They all marched steadily toward the river.

"Have we got another fight?" Matt asked quietly. "We're outnumbered, but could still take them on —"

"Oh, no," Shannahan said cheerfully. "It's just my boss, Clarence Hart, come to help me! Except you've already saved him the trouble!"

Sam and Matt stood side-by-side, where they could greet the newcomers and also keep an eye on Parrish, who was dripping on the riverbank and then stomping away from the scene. Others in his group were quietly retrieving their guns and disappearing into the night. Matt figured that he and Sam hadn't seen the last of Parrish, but that he would probably lay low for awhile, at least.

Hart stopped in front of the two brothers, looked them up and down, and then glanced at Shannahan.

"Well, William McFey Shannahan, I heard you were in trouble," Hart said. His voice was as big as he was. "I gather it wasn't with these two?"

"No, Mr. Hart," Shannahan answered. "I was in the river, doing my usual evening work for myself, as you encourage. And suddenly on the river was that new gunslick, Jack Parrish. He had me with my pants down, so to speak, when up came these two and evened the odds somewhat. I have to thank . . ." He paused and looked to Sam. "I don't even know your names!"

"He's Smith," Matt said. "I'm Jones."

"No, I'm Smith, and he's Jones," Sam corrected.

Hart raised one eyebrow at both of the two brothers, which caused them both to break out laughing.

"Oh, alright, you've got us," Matt said,

grinning. "It's an old joke, anyway. My name is Matt Bodine. That is Sam Two-Wolves."

"I've heard of you two," Hart said.

Sam rolled his eyes toward the sky. He said, "I think I preferred the days when nobody knew who we were!"

"Fame is the price we pay for being good!" Matt said.

Hart ignored the wisecracks and said, "I've heard you're good with guns. Are you looking for work?"

"No, we don't need the money," Matt said. "We're just drifting."

"Besides, if we were looking for work, we're more the ranching type, not the mining type," Sam said. "I have better things to do with my time than dig in wet gravel. And I have an aversion to being underground while I'm still breathing."

"Mining's not the work I had in mind." Hart motioned to his men. "I've got some good men, some honest, hard-working men. But that won't be enough. I need a couple of men who are good with a gun. Trouble's shaping up, and I'll need all the help I can get."

"And you think we could do the job?"

"I don't want anybody to get killed, on either side. I just want to protect my men, and let them do their jobs. You handled that situation a few minutes ago real nicely. And nobody got killed. I like your styles."

"Thanks for the compliment," Sam said. "But we don't hire out our guns. We may fight if we think the fight's worthwhile, but it's never for money."

"We would be willing to listen to your story over a few beers," Matt added. "I have a feeling we walked into a hornet's nest, and it might be a good idea to find out more about what all the buzzing's about."

"We'll listen to your story, then decide if we'll stay around for awhile or ride on."

Hart's face finally broke into a smile.

"In that case," he said, "the first round is on me!"

CHAPTER THREE

Outside the window was the picture of an 1870s mining operation: rock crusher, smelter, piles of rubble and men still at work. Inside was the picture of luxury: large desk, padded leather chairs, and Nelson Jordan, dressed in an expensive Eastern suit, smoking a large cigar. He was surprisingly young, not more than the mid-20s, leaning back in his chair, puffing the cigar as the three men in front of him shifted uncomfortably from foot to foot.

"So what happened?" Jordan asked. "Did you teach our pig-headed Irish friends a lesson?"

"Not exactly," the man on the right said. He was big, thick-bodied, with black curly hair.

"What do you mean . . . 'not exactly'?" Jordan said.

"Parrish was handling himself well until these two strangers came along . . ."

Jordan blew out some cigar smoke and asked in a deceptively mild voice, "And then what happened?"

"And the Irishman got away."

"Well, well. Parrish, what have you got to say about this?"

"They got the jump on me . . ." Parrish started. His clothes were still dripping with river water. His hat was soggy and his boots squeaked as he stood.

"Shut up!" Jordan suddenly roared, his voice filling the room. "I already know what happened. I don't want any panty-waist excuses."

Parrish's face turned purple, and he started to reach for his gun. The two large men on either side of him took a step closer to him, touched his arms. It was warning enough, and Parrish again dropped his hands.

"I expected much more from you, Parrish. You were supposed to be good with a gun and good with your fists. You were hired to do a job. I expected you to do the job."

"There were two of them, and one of me," Parrish said.

"But it only took one of them to beat you."

The man on the left now spoke. He was a little shorter and rounder, but still looked as if he could take care of himself in a brawl.

"Mr. Jordan, to Parrish's credit, it was a fair fight, except for one thing."

"And what's that, Grant?"

"The man Parrish fought is Sam Two-Wolves."

"So?"

"Him and his brother are top guns. They've been in lots of fights, and whipped butt in all of them. They fight and shoot like the devil himself. And they caught Parrish unexpected."

"That's right," Parrish agreed. "And when they got the jump on me . . ."

Jordan blew a smoke ring and said with a deadly chill, "I don't care if it is the devil himself. I hired you to do a job. Obviously you are inadequate for the job. You're fired."

Parrish's face turned even redder.

"You can't do that! I've traveled a long ways to work for you." Ignoring the cold looks on either side of him, Parrish continued, "I expect my pay in full, in gold or silver . . ."

Jordan tossed a small wad of paper money at him.

"You're luck I'm paying you this. It's more than you're worth. I recommend you make yourself scarce around these parts. If Two-Wolves and his brother don't get you, I might. Now get out of here."

Parrish looked as if he might challenge his former boss again, but decided against it. He pocketed the money and stomped out of the office, slamming the door behind him.

Jordan ignored the crash and continued to question his men.

"So what's the low-down on these two yahoos. Are they really gunfighters?"

"Sam Two-Wolves and Matt Bodine are some of the best," Grant said.

"Are they working for Hart?"

"Could be. Word has it that Hart was looking to recruit some guns. I haven't heard though about Bodine and Two-Wolves hiring out their guns. From what I hear about them, they're not for hire. Doesn't mean it couldn't happen. Enough silver and gold could buy anybody."

"I don't know if Hart has enough gold to buy top guns, but they sure sided with him without any hesitation," Jordan said.

The other man spoke up. "Could be another reason," he said.

"Look, Strep, what other reason could there be?"

"Those two also have a reputation for sticking their noses in where they don't belong. Maybe they were just looking for a little fun. Two-Wolves didn't even work up a· sweat. It may have been a little workout for him. He's a half-breed. Who knows how Indians think?"

"So what do you think? Should I have them killed?"

"As good as we are, Mr. Jordan, it would take a lot more of us to beat those two," Strep said. "If they're on Hart's side, they'll make it known soon enough. By then we'll have enough guns in town to match them. And if they're just passing through, we'll just let them pass."

Jordan flicked ashes from his cigar as he made the decision.

"Very well. Just keep an eye on them. Let me know what they're up to." He put the cigar back in his mouth. "By the way, have either of you two seen Malinda?"

"Not today," Grant said.

Strep shrugged.

"It's about showtime. I've warned her about being so lackadaisical about her comings and goings."

"Don't worry, boss. She'll show. She always does."

Jordan smiled.

"Yes," he said. "She always does."

Shannahan was doctoring his wounds with raw whiskey. He alternatively doused the gashes caused by the bullwhip with the alcohol and took big swallows from the bottle. Another bottle was being passed around, but Matt and Sam held beers.

The little saloon was hot and crowded with men much like Hart and his workers. The bar and tables were little more than rough planks and the sawdust on the floor had been well-used and packed down. Even so, the din of the talk of hard-working men was pleasant. And if the place was a little rough, it was nothing compared to some of the places the blood-brothers had seen.

"I still don't understand why you helped me," Shannahan said between dousings and swallows. "I don't know you from Adam."

"I like a fair fight," Sam said. "Two guns and a bullwhip against an unarmed man in a river isn't a fair fight."

"It's something to do with the innate honor of the noble savage," Matt said.

"You keep it up, and this noble will savage you," Sam answered.

Both men, however, were smiling as they traded insults and drank their beers.

"Seriously," Matt continued, motioning for another round of beers to the small bartender. "What's going on here? Isn't there any city marshal? Or has the law already been bought and paid for?"

Hart shook his head. He was also drinking beer. "This town is so new it might not even be called a real town. It has no town council. It has no laws and nobody to enforce them. All it's got is some of the richest gold and silver ore I've seen. The vein I'm trying to locate exactly and start working is silver, but there's gold here, too. You could almost go to any part of the river and start collecting dust. And now lots of men are trying to grab as much of the riches as they can, before going to the next strike. I was one of the first men here to stake claims. I originally just had to deal with the usual type of scum that show up at places like this. Claim jumpers. Robbers. Thugs of all kinds. But I've been in this business for a long time, and can hold my own against just about anybody. I managed to get some men together, and some equipment, and start some serious mining."

"And now you're rich?" Matt asked.

"No. I've got most of my money tied up in equipment and fancy big-city lawyers in the capital trying to protect my original claims. Sam, the man you beat earlier is Jack Parrish, a gunfighter hired by Nelson Jordan."

"Is Jordan another would-be claim-jumper?"

"Worse. Jordan is one of the lawyers that

had been working for me. He somehow twisted some deeds around and got himself a toe-hold here. He's got tons of money to invest, and has been slowly buying or taking over all the area around my claims, trying to squeeze me out. He's brought in the best mining talent money can buy and has a big operation. But he still hasn't managed to lay his hands on my claims, which are on the richest deposits here. He couldn't squeeze me out, and he couldn't buy me out. So now he's trying to force me out by bringing in his hired guns, harassing my men. I wouldn't be surprised if he didn't start some killing. That's why I offered to hire you two. My men need some protection."

The bartender brought over the fresh beers. Matt noticed with approval that in spite of the humble appearance of the saloon, the glasses and the rag over the bartender's shoulder were clean. Though for most of his life he had slept on the ground with only blankets between him and the stars, he still liked a clean glass for his beer.

"You might try sticking together a little closer," Sam said. "And maybe prepare yourselves for a fight at any time. After all, Shannahan all by himself without a weapon of any kind left him in the open."

Hart nodded. "We are prepared, up to a point. I try to keep my men working in teams, with at least one standing guard while the others work. It's a waste of good men, but it's better than getting them killed. I allow my men, however, to work certain parts of my claims for their own benefit."

Matt raised an eyebrow in question.

Hart continued, "I've been involved in mining for a long time. Believe me, there are more ways than you can imagine to steal from a claim or a mining company. Rather than waste all of my time trying to fight thefts, I let my men have a stake in the work — in addition to their pay. This operation is mainly involved with silver — there's not enough gold to make large-scale mining profitable. But there's enough for a single man to make money. So Shannahan and the others take an hour or so a day to work on their own, which would make groups a little awkward, don't you think?"

"You've developed an interesting concept to labor," Sam said. "That's not the method they teach back East."

"This is the West," Hart said. "We make our own rules by necessity."

Matt stretched and looked at Sam. "We can understand that. We've been known to make a few rules of our own."

"We're not partial to taking sides, but we just might stay in town for awhile," Sam added. "Just to kind of see what happens."

"We could always use a little entertainment," Matt concluded.

Shannahan took another drink, smiled broadly. Even though most of the bottle was gone, his words were still clear and his eyes were bright.

"Entertainment?" he said. "You boys want entertainment? Then you came to the right place!" Hart scowled, but Shannahan continued. "Jordan owns another saloon here in town. He has a singer there — Malinda Melody — and she puts on quite a show. She always plays to a packed house."

Sam looked to the sky and said, "Malinda Melody? Are you serious?"

"It's a stage name," Matt said. "You know, like the actresses do back East."

Hart scowled again. "Jordan brought the woman with him when he came to town. From the beginning, she's packed in the crowds — including my men, at first. Since the trouble started between Jordan's bunch and me, most of my men have avoided the place."

"To avoid fights?" Matt asked.

"No. We have a problem with using our

hard-earned money to enrich Jordan. I don't know why Shannahan even brought up the subject."

"Just being friendly," Shannahan said with a twinkle in his eye. "These two look like they could appreciate the sight of a pretty woman, and they might be able to meet Jordan in person and draw their own conclusions!"

"Good idea!" Sam said.

Matt almost spilled his beer. He asked, "Have you lost your mind? Jordan's men will be gunning for us anyway. Combine that with a hundred half-drunk and love-starved miners mooning over the only available woman for a hundred miles. And what does that give us?"

"An interesting evening?" Sam said with a deadpan expression on his face.

"That might be more entertainment than we really need," Matt suggested.

"Can you really resist seeing a woman named Malinda Melody?"

Matt laughed, finished his beer and put the empty glass on the table.

"Damn, I do like your philosophy of life," he said.

Outside of Jordan's office, Parrish stopped, pulled each of his revolvers to check their actions and to reload. They would need a thorough cleaning, but he had some fresh ammunition in his saddlebags.

When Parrish left Jordan's office, he had no intention of leaving town. It was bad enough to be humiliated by the half-breed, Two-Wolves. It was worse to be talked down to by a young pup like Jordan. So what if he had money and power? It was still only a two-bit mining town, and Parrish couldn't get by talking to Jack Parrish that way! If he left now, the story would be across the West in a matter of weeks, maybe even days. He would be a laughingstock, unable to get any more jobs. He could not let that happen.

Parrish felt the small wad of paper money that Jordan had tossed at him. Jordan had gold and silver running out of his ears. It didn't seem right that he should have all those riches and not share a little.

Parrish decided to find a way to correct that situation.

Fortunately, he had in his gear another bullwhip, which he would use when the time came. It would require some thought and planning, but he would find a way to teach both Sam Two-Wolves and Nelson Jordan a lesson they wouldn't forget!

And in so doing perhaps direct some of Nelson's gold and silver into Parrish's outstretched arms.

Parrish slipped his revolvers back into their holsters, straightened out his damp clothes as best as possible, repositioned his black hat on his head.

He smiled as he slipped into the night.

CHAPTER FOUR

Night had fallen, but the small mining town seemed as restless as ever. Rowdy voices drifted from saloons. Miners and drifters and card sharps walked from saloon to saloon. An occasional fight sounded from the alleys between the saloons. Coal-oil lamps or crude candles lighted the interiors of the buildings.

"Can't say this compares favorably to San Francisco," Matt said.

"Can't say it even compares favorably to any place I've ever been," Sam answered.

The two brothers had left Hart and his men talking easily among themselves to make their way to Nelson Jordan's saloon. The town, like most of the boom mining towns of the period, was composed mainly of ramshackle buildings hastily thrown together along streets that were little more than mud in wet weather and dust in dry weather.

The building containing Jordan's saloon on the outside resembled most of the others in the ramshackle town and looked as if a solid wind would blow it away.

"The only thing coming close to class is the two-color sign," Matt said, pointing to the area of the building above the door reading, "Jordan's Saloon and Opera House." The sign was red and the letters were in green.

A line had already formed and was rapidly moving inside.

"Think there'll be any tickets left?" Matt asked.

"You mean you think they'd really sell *us* tickets?"

"I'm ever the optimist."

"Yeah. You probably even expect this Malinda Melody to be pretty."

"Worse. I expect her to really be able to carry a tune!"

The two men laughed. As Sam reached the ticket window, some of the miners, overhearing the conversation, started their own rumblings under their breath.

The ticket seller scowled at the blood-brothers, but finally said, "Twenty-five dollars. Each."

"Ouch."

"The show is included. The drinks

are extra."

Sam looked back at Matt. "Well, brother?"

Matt shrugged. "Not much else going on in town tonight." He reached into his pocket, pulled out a small bag and removed some gold coins. "Here. This should cover us."

The ticket taker scowled again, but quickly pocketed the money.

The inside of the building was a variation of the typical saloon. It was bigger than most, with a small stage at the rear. A bar extended down either side. Lighting was provided by lamps hanging from the walls and ceilings and along the stage. The heat combined with too many bodies in too small an area. Most of those in attendance didn't seem to mind the uncomfortable facilities as they crowded around the bars and pushed each other for positions closest to the stage.

Sam and Matt also elbowed their way through the crowd. After a few minutes, Sam glanced behind him and said softly, "We're being followed."

"How can you tell in this crowd?"

Sam motioned behind and around them. The men who had watched them earlier were still talking among themselves but were now encircling the brothers. As they approached, others in the crowd stepped the other way, as if sensing trouble was about to break out.

"Ambush? Jordan's men?" Matt asked under his breath.

"That's what I don't understand. They don't look like they'd be Jordan's men. They're not gunfighters. Some of them aren't even wearing guns."

"Yeah, I noticed that, too. Seems kind of peculiar."

In only a few minutes, it was obvious that the blood brothers were being encircled. Even in the crowded saloon, a space had formed around them. One of the men at the edge of the circle took another drink and finally spoke. He said loudly, "I heard you making fun of Miss Melody!" He was tall, bearded, and looked as if he hadn't had a bath in months. His eyes were small and mean, as if they were filled with hate.

The man next to him punched him lightly in the arm and said, "You tell him, Rex."

But Rex wasn't laughing or smiling. "Don't deny it. We all heard it. You owe an apology to Miss Melody."

Sam rolled his eyes toward the ceiling, tilting his head back slightly, revealing the Indian necklace around his neck.

Rex spotted it, and said, "Nobody has a right to talk that way about Miss Melody.

Especially an *Injun."*

In spite of the crowded conditions, the small space around Matt and Sam was quickly cleared.

"Pardon me," Matt said. "But you have it wrong."

"Only Injuns wear that jewelry."

Matt pulled his own necklace out from under his shirt. "Wrong. About everything. I'm the one who was talking about your entertainer. And it wasn't intended as an insult. I think it is you who owe Sam an apology."

"Like hell." Rex swung his glass at Matt, who ducked underneath the swing. He punched the other man in the stomach, doubling him over, then stood quickly, flipping him backwards.

Sam, knowing from long experience working with Matt how he fought, at the same time kicked out at the man standing next to Rex. The kick caught him in the chest, forcing him backwards as well.

Both men landed with thuds, but were quickly up again as others rushed to their aid.

Two jumped at Matt, who sidestepped them, causing the two attackers to hit against each other. As they fell, Matt doubled his fists and brought them down on the backs of their necks.

Three men attacked Sam. One tried to pin his arms, to allow the other two a chance to give a good beating. However, the hold was not solid. Sam twisted, got one arm free, and brought his elbow backwards, giving a bruising hit to his captor just below his ribs, knocking the breath out of him. Sam then pivoted and with the same motion brought a left upwards, hitting the other man's face and throwing him with full force at the third man.

Matt backhanded another miner trying to sneak up behind him. The man stiffened and fell like a pole-axed ox, tripping up another would-be attacker behind him. Matt captured the tripped-up attacker by the back of his shirt and hurled him toward Sam.

Sam grabbed the man nearest him by the back of his shirt and hurled him toward Matt.

The two mine workers seemed to sail through the air, colliding with each other halfway between the brothers.

Rex had now recovered enough to reach for his revolver. Almost as one, Matt and Sam pulled their own revolvers so quickly that the movements were barely a blur, though Matt was slightly faster. The guns were in their hands before Rex's had even cleared leather.

Suddenly staring down the barrels of two large hand guns sobered Rex up quickly.

"No . . . no need to shoot," he said. "I guess I did misunderstand."

Matt and Sam weren't in the habit of shooting men unless it was a fair fight, and drawing against a drunken miner was hardly fair. They weren't going to shoot in any case, though the man on stage didn't know that. In a loud voice, he called out, "That's enough fun! You boys just quiet down now and get ready for the show!"

Rex, now staring at the two large guns just feet from his face, swallowed hard. He said, "Right, Mr. Jordan."

"I think the misunderstanding has been cleared up," Sam said.

"You boys can continue your fun if you want — outside, after the show," Jordan said.

As Matt and Sam holstered their guns, Rex said softly, "I'll continue it later. You can count on it."

"It's no business of mine," Jordan continued. "Now, however, it is my pleasure to present to you the one and only — Malinda Melody!"

The fight — even the guns in the hands of

Matt and Sam — was suddenly forgotten as the men in the bar stared toward the stage. It became so quiet that even the dripping of the beer taps could be heard.

A young woman walked onto the stage with a smooth grace. She was dressed in a stunning white gown. Her brown hair was styled in tight curls. In spite of the poor lighting, she seemed to fill the stage with her presence.

Matt's mouth dropped open as he watched the entrance.

Sam saw the expression on his brother's face and said, "Great. I recognize that look."

Matt said, "Sssh. I want to see this."

"Wonderful. You're going to fall for this girl and get us all in a helluva lot of trouble."

"Sssh."

Malinda started to sing. There was no background music, no supporting cast, no fancy lighting. There was just the woman and her singing. The songs were not fancy, and certainly not opera. But by the third note she had the woman-hungry men in the audience eating out of her hand.

"Such a wonderful singer!" Matt said.

"A little better than a squeaky wagon wheel, not quite as good as a mockingbird," Sam answered, expecting to get an argument. In reality, he had to admit Malinda had a fairly strong voice and a natural feel for the music, but he wanted to needle his brother. Matt ignored the remark, watching the woman move across the stage. A hundred sets of eyes followed her. Her dress was far less revealing than most saloon performers wore, but on her it was suggestive of forbidden fun. The fantasies induced in the minds of the miners were perhaps more entertaining than the songs being sung.

As Malinda finished each song, the formerly quiet bar erupted into a thunderous chorus of applause that grew louder after each song. The men whistled and yelled and cried out for more. After about six songs, Malinda blew a kiss, causing the men to cheer even more.

"Quite a talent, don't you think?" a confident voice said behind Sam.

He pivoted quickly, hand on his revolver, then paused.

Nelson Jordan stood next to the bar, both hands in plain sight, smiling broadly, smoking an expensive cigar.

As Malinda left the stage, to still more cheers, Matt also turned. The crowd had moved toward the stage, temporarily giving a little more space to Jordan, Sam, and Matt.

"Don't tell me," Jordan said. "You're Sam Two-Wolves and Matt Bodine. I've already heard about your run-in with one of my former employees."

"Former employees?"

"Jack Parrish had worked for me. But what he was doing to that man in the river was uncalled for, don't you think? So I fired him."

Sam and Matt did not take their eyes off Jordan as he smoked. He blew a smoke ring and asked, "So what do you think of our local heroine?"

"Fair to middlin'," Sam said.

"Yeah, and you're a better judge of horse-flesh than woman-flesh," Matt said.

"Too skinny for my taste."

"But not for these lonely miners," Jordan added. "To them, who live in a world where any woman, even a whore, is fairly rare, seeing a real woman like Malinda is a bargain at any price. I'm a businessman. I'm just providing a service."

"I bet you provide a lot more services than singing."

Jordan shrugged. "Like I said, I'm a businessman." He paused, then continued, "Speaking of service, I could use a few more men like you. I like the way you handled Parrish. I saw the way you took care of the

50

troublemakers earlier this evening. And I admire your guts — being Hart's men, and coming into my place this way. Whatever he's paying you, I can double."

"Our guns aren't for sale," Matt said.

"Aren't they?" Jordan's voice suddenly grew stern. "You came pretty quickly to the aid of Hart's men. It's no secret that we're both recruiting. You think I was born yesterday?"

"We don't work for Hart," Sam said. "We don't work for you. We're just a couple of drifters looking for a little entertainment."

Jordan blew another smoke ring.

"Is that so? Well, boys, I'd recommend you move on, in case you're tempted to take the wrong side. Just because you boys are good doesn't mean you can't be beat."

"We also don't take to threats."

"Not a threat, boys. Just a little friendly advice. But because I've got a big heart, I'll let you watch the rest of the show."

"Oh, thank you *so much,*" Sam said with mock sincerity. His comment, however, was lost on Jordan, who was now also watching the stage as Malinda returned for her next number.

Matt continued to watch Jordan, then moved behind him so that he could watch him as well as the woman on stage. Sam also moved slightly, but Jordan had apparently dismissed him and Matt, and had his mind on the woman or possibly some of his other business dealings.

Jack Parrish remained seated on his horse in an alley a few blocks from Jordan's Saloon and Opera House. He had been waiting there patiently for most of the evening.

He had watched Sam and Matt stand in line and enter the building.

He had watched Malinda ride up to the side of the building in her fancy buckboard, and then as she and Jordan talked angrily to each other.

Parrish had then moved closer to the saloon, where he had heard the faint echoes of a fight from inside the building, and then the voice of the girl as she started her show. Through an open door, he had watched as Matt became entranced with the girl, and listened as Jordan talked briefly to the brothers.

Under cover of darkness, he quickly went back to his hiding place in the alley, until the show was over and the crowd started to stream back into the street.

He watched as the girl and one of Jordan's men, the one called Strep, left by the side entrance. They quickly got into the buckboard and started down the street.

Parrish clucked softly to his horse and followed at a discreet distance.

He expected the buckboard to take the couple back to Jordan's hotel, where Malinda was living. It was common knowledge that she was Jordan's girl. Parrish had also learned that the girl was not particularly fond of the barbaric town to which Jordan had brought her, and often took rides into the surrounding country to try and escape the ever present stench. So Parrish wasn't too surprised to see the buckboard continue past the hotel toward the edge of town. It turned before the tent city and moved toward the river.

Now Parrish kept a greater distance, but continued to keep the girl and her escort in sight. He noted the route taken, including the clearing by the river where the buckboard stopped and the girl got out and walked along the river for several minutes. As she walked, she threw rocks into the water, watching the concentric circles rippled outward.

Finally, the woman got back on the buckboard and her guard started the drive back into town.

Parrish had seen enough. He spurred his

horse in the opposite direction to return to town by another route and to finish devising his plan that would teach both the blood brothers and Nelson Jordan a lesson they would not soon forget!

CHAPTER FIVE

Even though Matt and Sam had remained in the saloon until very late, they were up at the crack of dawn. Each had slipped out of his bedroll before the sun had risen above the horizon, as refreshed with a few hours' sleep as most men would have been on a full night's sleep. The two blood brothers took turns with the camp chores. Today Sam was taking care of the horses, making sure they were watered and fed, while Matt tended to the cooking. By the time Sam had led the horses back from the river, Matt had the meat frying and the coffee boiling.

Sam walked over to the fire and poured himself a cup of coffee, making a face.

"You know my cooking's not that bad," Matt said, pretending to have hurt feelings.

"It's not your cooking, it's the water," Sam answered. "I thought we'd be far enough out of town to breathe some decent air and drink some clean water. No such luck."

"I had to travel quite a ways downstream to find clean enough water for the coffee," Matt agreed. "All things considered, I'd rather run cattle and horses than mess up the good earth with mining."

"You're talking more like an Indian than a white man," Sam said, crouching down by the fire and stabbing a slice of meat to his metal plate. "What happened to the idea of progress — meaning making the white men rich?"

"Don't forget I spent a lot of years with you and your father, learning Cheyenne ways. I can't fault any man for making a living or trying to get rich. But some ways are better than others." He poured coffee into his own cup. "Like the situation in this town. What do you make of it?"

"You know me. You know I follow my instincts. And I like Clarence Hart. He seems to be a solid, honest, hard-working man. And I liked the way Shannahan stood up to that gunfighter." He paused, a chunk of meat halfway between the plate and his mouth. "What do you think?"

"I think that Jordan and Parrish and the other gunfighters Jordan brought in could have easily been found under some of the rocks dredged up in Jordan's mining operation. It doesn't seem to be adding up to a very fair fight. It takes more than honesty and hard work to beat a Colt and a Winchester, especially when you've been bushwhacked."

"I think we should probably stick around awhile, just in case."

"I couldn't agree more."

Sam almost choked on his meat.

"You're singing a different tune than you were last night."

"Maybe I was playing devil's advocate."

"Like hell you were."

"Alright. Maybe I had a few doubts at first. But events last night helped to change my mind."

Sam chewed awhile, then understanding brought a twinkle to his dark eyes.

"I get it now. You're singing a different song because you have a tin ear and you've fallen for that mining camp songstress."

Matt answered somberly, "She's not *that* bad of a singer."

Sam answered, "No, I guess not. But if you had to fall for a woman, why couldn't it be somebody a little less . . . potentially troublesome."

"I like a challenge."

The talk was interrupted by the sound of a horse and a loud voice calling out, "Hello in the camp!"

"Come on in, Hart!" Sam said. "We've got plenty of grub!"

Clarence Hart, riding a large black horse, broke through the brushes and into the camp. Hart easily dismounted and tied his mount near the other horses. Today he was wearing a shirt and a narrow-brimmed felt hat.

"How'd you know where to find us?" Matt asked, pouring a cup of coffee for the third man.

"A process of elimination," Hart answered. "The only hotel is owned by Jordan, and you and he are not necessarily on good speaking terms. I figured you preferred to camp out in the open, and I knew this was one of the better spots in the area. Before the water got so bad, I used to fish out here a lot. I figured you'd find this place. Turns out I was right." He took a sip of coffee, and smiled. "Hey, this isn't bad coffee to be made by a cowboy!"

"Yeah, and you ought to see the way he sweeps the floor!" Sam said.

Matt threw the dregs from his coffee cup at Sam, who dodged easily. Both men laughed.

Hart crouched down around the fire with the two brothers and said more seriously, "You know why I came up here to see you.

I wondered if you've thought any more about my proposition."

"Yes, we have," Sam answered. "No, our guns still aren't for sale. On that point there is no argument."

Hart sighed. "Very well. My men and I have survived this long. We'll find a way to survive this fight, as well." He started to stand. "I thank you for the coffee, and for the help you gave my man yesterday. Now, I'll be on my way . . ."

Sam reached out and touched the Irishman lightly on the arm. "Don't jump to conclusions. I said we don't hire out our guns. But we will fight for a good cause. We decided to stick around for awhile, just in case you need a little back-up. We haven't run across too many honest men in our travels. You'd be good for this country. A lot better than men like Jordan."

Hart shook his head slightly. "Some might say you boys are a little touched in the head. But I have to admire men who put their action where their hearts are at. I'm glad you're staying around."

"Oh, it's not entirely altruistic," Sam said. "Matt has reasons of his own. He has his eyes set on a little songbird in your town."

"Not Malinda Melody!"

Matt looked a little sheepish, which was

confirmation enough for Hart.

Sam laughed, but Hart's face was again somber.

"I make it a point to never tell another man how to live his life or conduct his business, especially where women are concerned," Hart said. "But I've got to warn you about this one. Malinda is Jordan's property as much as if he owned her. He shows her off on the stage of his saloon, but nobody can get near her off the stage. Several have tried. None have succeeded."

"Point taken," Matt said. He stood, placed his cup in his saddlebags, and then started to saddle his horse, whistling a faint tune.

"Where you headed?" Hart asked.

"Need you ask?" Sam said.

Matt stepped into the stirrup and tossed his long leg over the horse's back.

"If you need me, I'll be in town, doing a little sparking," Matt said.

"Like I said, it's none of my business," Hart said, his somber face breaking into a smile. "She lives in Jordan's hotel. And may good luck ride with you!"

Matt tipped his hat and started his horse on a trot back into town.

As he watched Matt ride into the woods, Hart said to Sam, "You know, I just bet he might do it!"

"No bets. If I know Matt, he'll find some clever way of meeting the woman. Hell if I know what women see in him." Then, suddenly snapping to attention, Sam said, "Hey! He rode off without breaking camp! And that was his job today! No wonder he was whistling!"

Hart laughed.

Nelson Jordan, as always, was wearing an expensive suit, even though he was on the riverbank looking over some potential sites where the silver ore might be buried.

"Dammit, Smithson, I want results!" he yelled, the lit cigar in his hand making wide circles. "I'm paying you damned good money, so where's the vein?"

The mining engineer pointed to a geological chart in his hand and said, "We're getting close. These marked spots are the areas that have the best potential. The circled spots are where we've already done some exploration and some mining activity is taking place. But nothing is certain. And look —" He tapped the paper with a dirty finger. "The best spots are still on land held by Hart."

Jordan put the cigar back in his mouth and puffed angrily. "So tell me something I don't know. I'm paying you to find a way around this. The vein must curve around and hit my land at some point."

"I can only do what's scientifically possible," Smithson responded. "And let's face it, Hart's facing the same problems we are."

"Like what?"

"Like he can only do so much exploration, and with his limited resources he can't hit as many areas at one time as we can. And he has to fight the river just as we do."

Jordan started to puff less angrily. "Let's see that map again."

Smithson spread it out on the ground. "Look, here is the river. Here are some of the feeder channels leading to it, crossing right over where some of the potential sites are located. Here is where we've managed to dam some of the flow, and here is where Hart's men are working. We have better pumps than they have, we have more men than Hart has. But we're all fighting the same battle."

"Hmm. What if the dam gives way?"

"We'd both lose a lot of work."

"Yes. But we could probably recover faster. And in fact it might ruin Hart's operation." Jordan was now puffing contentedly, the smoke rising in a faint cloud around his face. "You've done good work, Smithson. But I wonder if you might have better luck trying some different sites." Jordan pointed to a different spot on the map.

"But that's up in the hills, and based on the geological strata, the chances of finding ore is much slimmer . . ."

Jordan lifted his hand to stop the flow of words. "I just have a feeling. Trust me on this one. You just get my men, and my more valuable equipment, up there."

"If you say so, Mr. Jordan."

"Trust me on this one."

Matt Bodine rode slowly into the town that was called, almost by default, Jordanville. In the daylight, it looked even more dingy than it had the night before. The streets were nearly deserted, as the men were all along the river or in the mines, searching for the buried treasure of gold and silver ore.

Matt was still whistling softly to himself, full of good humor, though he wasn't sure why. He had mainly been joking with Sam about his intent to woo Malinda, but it was an idea that had taken hold in his mind and wouldn't let go. It was true that in his travels he had seen many good-looking women, some of them far more beautiful than the mining-town singer. Matt had been with a fair number of them, though none had ever convinced him to give up his wandering life to settle down, or to even stay for more than a short time. For some reason, however, he felt a strong attraction to Malinda, even though they had never met.

He was sure he could find a way for their paths to cross before the day was over.

Though the town at this time of day was relatively quiet, Matt watched the area around him with experienced eyes. Most of the buildings were only one story high, and there were no good hiding places for a would-be bushwhacker. Matt passed the saloon where Malinda had sung the night before. Some men were inside drinking and playing cards. These would be some of the riff-raff that frequented every mining town, trying to fleece the hard-working miners of their hard-earned money.

Soon, the Hotel Jordan came into view. It appeared to be slightly more substantial, with two stories and a porch on the front and a plank sidewalk extending in front of it. The lots on both sides of it were vacant, as if in anticipation of future growth.

Matt stopped his horse to look over the hotel and figure his next move and how he could arrange a meeting with Malinda.

Suddenly the hairs on the back of his neck seemed to tingle and he sensed rather than saw the glint of morning sunlight off the gun barrel on the roof of the hotel. Matt spurred his horse and dropped his head to the horse's neck as the shot rang out. The bullet whizzed past the spot where Matt had been just seconds before.

Matt urged his mount toward the hotel at full speed. Without slowing the horse, the young adventurer slipped his right foot out of the saddle and leaped toward the ground.

Another shot rang out. This one was even farther from its mark than the first one had been.

Matt rolled in the dusty street behind a horse trough, pulling his own revolver. He shot twice toward the area from where the attack had come. Matt had no illusions that one of his bullets would find its intended target, but it might put his attacker on the defensive. The bullets sent splinters flying, but did no other damage.

The horse rushing toward the hotel was a different matter. It could not stop in time, and crashed into the porch. It panicked, reared on its hind legs, and brought its front legs down through the front wall.

Suddenly there were men swarming out of the hotel as Matt's horse turned and ran in the opposite direction. They were all cursing and screaming at the unfortunate animal. If they were aware of the shooting, they gave no indication of it, and they apparently did not see Matt.

No other shots came from the roof, so Matt raced from behind the water trough to a corner of the porch roof. He holstered his gun to get a better grip on the rafters. The men now yelling among themselves about the damaged hotel front did not even notice Matt as he jumped up and with an easy athletic grace, spun himself to the porch roof and pulled his gun again. The roof was at a slight pitch, making it easy for him to run across it toward where the shots had come from — a higher part of the roof that covered the hotel itself. He moved slowly at first, until he was sure that he was not making himself an easy target and that the roof was strong enough to hold him.

Matt looked around, wondering if he had missed his attacker. He got his answer when another shot was fired from behind a chimney. Matt fell to the roof, returned the fire, and moved toward the chimney. He circled it in time to see only a blur of black going toward the rear of the building. Matt shot again, and gave chase, his footsteps echoing loudly into the hotel below.

In the few seconds it took Matt to cross the length of the roof, his attacker had made it to the edge and was making his escape.

At the rear of the building, a black hat was descending almost out of sight toward the ground and a pair of hands was holding onto the roof.

"Stop!" Matt said. "I've got you covered. Don't move and I'll let you live."

One hand let go and the other was about to do the same. Matt thought quickly, and decided he could let the man drop to the ground, where he would be an easy target from the high vantage point of the roof.

The second hand let go, and Matt heard the soft plop as the man landed on the ground below.

Matt took a quick step, when he heard a faint crunching sound. His foot hit a rotten part of the roof, causing it to cave in on him.

Matt rolled himself in a ball and tried to land as softly as he could.

To his surprise, he landed not on hard plank flooring or dirt, but on a large bed.

Through the dust swirling around him, he saw one of the most beautiful — and unexpected — sights he had seen in years.

Malinda Melody was in a large, steaming bathtub, wearing nothing but soapsuds and a confused look in her eyes.

CHAPTER SIX

Falling through the roof into Malinda Melody's room while she was taking a bath was Matt Bodine's first surprise.

That she did not react like what he considered a typical hysterical female was his second surprise.

It was difficult to maintain his dignity after he had fallen on his rear with dust still swirling around him, but Matt did the best he could. He rolled quickly off the bed, took off his hat, and introduced himself.

"Good morning, ma'am," he said, bowing slightly. "My name is Matthew Bodine, and I'm quite a fan of yours. I apologize for crashing in on you like this."

Malinda was even prettier in person than she had been on the stage of Jordan's saloon the night before. Her eyes were a deep shade of blue. Her brown hair, which had been arranged in tight curls the night before, now hung loosely around her lovely face. Her skin was smooth, almost the color of ivory with touches of pink in the cheeks. Matt wished that the soapsuds were not quite so thick so that he could see more of the woman than just her head, neck, and bare arms.

"I've had many men approach me, but never in a way quite this direct." She was smiling as she talked. "You realize, of course, you're taking quite a chance. When Jordan's men find you here, you'll be going out the door — feet first, headed for a grave."

Outside the door, Matt heard voices and footsteps. He figured he had only a few minutes before Jordan's men figured out where he had gone. He considered his rather limited options. He could try to escape the way he came in, except that the hotel was probably now surrounded. He could try to shoot his way out. This was tempting, since he was still all fired up about one of Jordan's men taking potshots at him from the hotel rooftop. On the other hand, if it was Jordan trying to kill him, why hadn't there been a more organized attempt? Jordan didn't seem like the kind of man to allow a loose cannon in his organization.

Maybe there was a third option?

"Well, ma'am, if I must die, then I can die a happy man. I can say that my eyes have seen the most beautiful woman from California to St. Louis!"

Malinda's smile grew even larger.

"You look like a cowboy, but you talk like a gentleman."

"Don't ever underestimate a cowboy, ma'am. We can probably appreciate a fine woman more than any Easterner, and we have talents that would surprise you. If you could find it in your heart to forgive me for this intrusion, and make it up to you with dinner tonight, I could surely appreciate it."

Malinda cocked her head to one side, used her right hand to pull her hair back. The bubbles started to slide down her arm suggestively, but still only far enough to suggest the delights hidden below the water.

"Just how much of a gentleman are you, Mr. Matthew Bodine?"

"Call me Matt."

The woman laughed. "Very well, Matt. You can call me Malinda." She motioned at him with her finger to come closer. "I could use some help out of the tub. But, please, you must keep your head turned and your eyes closed."

It was Matt's turn to laugh.

"Who would believe it? I'm with the most

beautiful woman I've ever seen, in her bath, and she asks me to close my eyes to the beauty!"

"If you are a gentleman . . ."

Outside the door, voices were louder and footsteps were pounding down the hall.

"You have my word as a gentleman that I shall avoid the temptation to look."

True to his word, Matt turned his head and closed his eyes even as Malinda pulled herself out of the tub, wrapped a large towel around herself and disappeared behind a large curtain dividing the room.

When he heard the woman close the curtain, Matt started to pull out his Colt, then changed his mind. He wanted to avoid shooting in such tight quarters, if possible. A stray bullet could accidently hit the woman behind the curtain, humming softly to herself.

Matt placed his gun back in its holster and took a position to one side of the door.

A rough voice called out, "Malinda! Are you alright?"

Without waiting for an answer, the door crashed open and three men rushed in with guns drawn.

As Jack Parrish approached Hart's camp, canvas bag in hand, he considered his morning's work. He felt he had at least partly met his goal adding fuel to the already hot fire between Hart and Jordan and maneuvering Matt Bodine and Sam Two-Wolves into the fray.

On the other hand, he had seriously underestimated Matt Bodine.

Parrish hadn't really wanted to kill the stranger, since the gunfighter's feud was with Bodine's blood brother, Sam Two-Wolves. The two men, however, seemed as much of a matched team as Parrish had ever seen, which meant that an attack on one would be an attack on the other. By taking shots at him from the top of Jordan's building, Parrish had hoped to make Bodine think that Jordan was trying to have him killed. If this led to Bodine killing Jordan, or the other way around, made no difference to Parrish. He just wanted to muddy the waters and get some bullets flying from both sides. In the end, Hart, aided by the blood brothers, and Jordan would destroy each other, leaving Parrish to come in and pick up the pieces.

Bodine, however, had reacted with surprising speed to the shots being fired at him. He went on the attack, and Parrish had almost gotten caught in return. A few of Bodine's shots had whizzed uncomfortably close to Parrish's ears. It was a lucky break that Bodine had fallen through a weak spot in the roof. Parrish had not waited around to see the end result of his efforts, but he figured it might even work out better than Parrish had planned! If Bodine was caught in the hotel, Jordan might think that it was Bodine who was the attacker, and kill him on the spot. That would really make the Two-Wolves bastard mad!

Parrish was now hiding in a stand of trees near the main supply shed for the Hart camp. His horse was safely tied close by in case he needed to make a fast escape. Inside the building were all the explosives needed to conduct a major mining project. So far, Hart had sunk just a few holes, looking for the exact spot that would lead to the main vein. When he hit the vein, he would be ready to move fast.

Elsewhere in the area, Jordan was starting similar projects, though even his deepest mine was still only large enough for a few men at a time.

Even so, Parrish knew both Jordan and Hart were making good money in these early stages of development.

The gunfighter moved a little closer, made sure nobody was nearby, then hurried to the door. It had a metal lock, but the door and frame were just wood and easily splintered under Parrish's efforts. He quickly slipped inside. He remained motionless while his eyes adjusted to the dim light.

Wooden boxes, mostly unmarked, were stacked high in the room. Parrish moved them around, trying to determine their contents. Finally, disgusted, he started to pry lids from the boxes. On the third try, he found what he was looking for — sticks of prepackaged explosive, ready for use. Parrish started to shove the explosive into his sack.

How much did he need? Parrish was more familiar with guns than explosives, but he knew enough to make a good educated guess. He also stuffed lengths of fuse and other necessary items into his sack.

Parrish tied the bag shut, walked to the door, and listened. All seemed to be quiet. The gunfighter cracked the door, then slipped out as quietly as he had entered.

The entire operation took only a few minutes.

Parrish chuckled softly as he thought about the next part of his plan.

Matt tripped up the first man coming through the door into Malinda Melody's room. As he fell to the floor, his feet got tangled up with the man behind him, who lost his balance and went flying head over heels, landing with a wet plop in the bathtub vacated just a few minutes before by the woman.

The third man was a little more cautious and held back when the first two men went down. He came into the room a little more slowly. As he inched into the room, Matt kicked. The toe of his boot caught the outstretched gun, also sending it flying across the room. Almost instantly, he grabbed the third man's arm and twisted it, forcing out an agonized groan.

Matt threw the third man to the floor and started for the door, when suddenly a dozen men were upon him. Matt kicked and clawed, breaking bones and noses, but in the end was forced to the floor through sheer weight of numbers. Two men were required to hold down each arm and leg.

"What do we have here, boys?"

The voice came from a large man in the doorway.

"Don't know him, Strep," one of the men answered. "He can put up one helluva fight. Think he's one of Hart's men?"

"Lift him up and let's take a look."

Strong hands pulled Matt from the floor. He relaxed his muscles slightly, waiting for an opening.

"I'm not one of Hart's men," Matt said. "We explained that to Jordan last night. So what's the big idea of taking potshots at me?"

Strep moved closer. "I recognize you now. You're partnered up with that Indian, Two-Wolves. I thought you were tougher than this. And smarter."

"Like hell. One of you bastards was shooting at me, and I shot back. Almost got him, too."

"So that's the story you're using? Well, I never gave no orders to shoot you. Think I may change my mind, now. Boys, teach him a lesson."

"No." The voice was as soft as a whisper but cut through the men more than a shouted order. "Let go of Mr. Bodine."

To Matt's amazement, the hands holding him suddenly loosened. Matt pulled loose, reached for his Colt, but paused in mid-draw as his eyes, along with all the others in the room, were pulled almost on their own to where Malinda had stepped out from behind the curtain. She was wearing a soft gown of some kind, her hair still damp from her bath and hanging loosely to her shoulders.

She was holding a shotgun, but it was her

voice, not the gun, that caused the men to listen to her.

"This man is a gentleman," Malinda said. "You men could take lessons from him in how to talk to a woman."

"Don't be foolish, Malinda," Strep said. He pointed at the hole in the ceiling. "Look at the facts. He tried to destroy Jordan's hotel. He attacked you by way of the roof. He's probably working for Hart." Strep looked down at the man in the bathtub, who was slowly regaining consciousness. "Looks like he may be a Peeping Tom, as well, watching you in your bath."

"Oh, Strep, you're just jealous you weren't the one who saw me in my awkward predicament."

Strep's face grew red, whether from anger or embarrassment Matt couldn't say.

"No matter. Jordan wouldn't like it."

"Wouldn't like what?" Jordan's voice came from the hallway. "Would somebody tell me what's going on in my hotel?"

Before anybody could answer, Matt had pushed his way through Jordan's men and had Jordan by his coat collar.

"You know damn well what's going on," Matt said. "Somebody tried to use me for target practice from the top of your hotel. I don't take kindly to being bushwhacked."

Strep and another of Jordan's men reached for their guns. Matt dropped to one knee, pivoted, and drew his own Colt. The shot was loud in the small room. The bullet caught the other man in the shoulder, forcing him backwards. Matt directed his gun toward Strep, who froze in mid-draw.

Jordan held up his right hand.

"No more shooting," he said. "Strep, put your gun away. All of you men put your guns away." His men hesitantly pushed their guns back into their holsters. "Get him to the doctor. I think he'll live. Had Bodine here wanted to kill somebody, he'd be dead now."

"Damned right," Matt said. "Now why don't you come clean with me, before somebody else gets hurt!"

Jordan took the cigar from his mouth with his right hand.

"Wasn't my man shooting at you," he said. "Like I explained last night, my fight's not with you and Two-Wolves. I'd rather you two leave Jordanville, the sooner the better. Why would I do something to get you riled?"

"And I'm to believe you?"

"To be fair, have you reason to call me a liar? I know you've talked with Hart. You know his opinion of me. But have I done anything to you that would justify your damaging my building and attacking my men?"

Matt placed his Colt back in its holster.

"Then who shot at me?"

Jordan shrugged.

"And I have a question for you. What are you doing with my star performer, in her bath? If I were a less reasonable man, I might have you shot for this offense alone."

"I believe his story," Malinda said. "He was making as much noise up there as a herd of buffalo, and I'm sure I heard two sets of footsteps. Attacking you and your men in broad daylight without provocation doesn't seem to be Mr. Bodine's style." Then she added, as if that settled the argument, "And he was a perfect gentleman with me."

Strep glared at the woman. Jordan's face was unreadable as he puffed on his cigar. Matt remained motionless, alert to even the hint of an attack. Malinda smiled innocently.

Finally, Jordan said, "Mr. Bodine, I may regret this decision, but at this point I'll give you the benefit of the doubt. Malinda for some reason seems to like you. So I won't try to detain you. I'll even help in whatever way I can to find the culprit who shot at you."

"You do what you have to do, and I'll do what I have to do," Matt answered. He walked to the door, paused, then turned to Malinda. He said, "How about that dinner tonight?"

"I'd be delighted. I'll see you then."

Matt tipped his hat and left the room.

CHAPTER SEVEN

Sam August Webster Two-Wolves spoke the truth when he said he was not particularly interested in mining, but he still agreed to take a tour of Jordanville and Hart's mining operations. Sam had a naturally keen mind, well-trained in the traditional Indian beliefs and skills that involved cooperation and interaction with the natural world. His mind had also been further developed by his attendance in the white man's colleges. He had done surprisingly well in the sciences as well as philosophy, and he carried over his interests past his college days. So Sam jumped at this chance to see the early stages of mining operations.

"There is a certain amount of gold to be found in the riverbed and on its banks," Hart said. "A person lucky enough, or willing to work long enough and hard enough, could earn a decent living for awhile. The real treasure, however, is buried within the earth. As a prospector, my job is to look at the clues that may lead to the main vein. As a mining engineer, my job would then be to find a way to sink a shaft deep enough, pull up enough ore-bearing dirt and then find a way to process the ore to yield enough metal to make pay for the costs of operations — and to make a profit."

Sam bent down, picked up some of the dirt between his fingers. It felt rocky, would probably be poor to yield growing things. Other than that, his examination provided little information.

"If I remember correctly, you face many problems even if you can find the main vein," Sam said. "You have engineering problems sinking the shaft, sometimes through solid rock, sometimes through sandy soil that caves in on itself. You have drainage and ventilation problems."

"And many more. That is why I have only started a few exploratory shafts. Jordan, more ambitious and more reckless, has one much deeper. You can see his digging equipment to your left."

Sam noted several people working at a rather leisurely pace on Jordan's side of the claim line. Sam had expected more men working at a faster pace. If anything, Jordan's men seemed to be moving supplies *away* from the mine.

"And this is your claim?" Sam said, letting the dirt run through his fingers.

"Yeah, he's kind of pushing the line, isn't he? I wouldn't be surprised if he doesn't try to direct his tunnel toward my claim. I don't know if anything he does would surprise me."

"Are you that certain that we're standing on buried treasure?"

"No. It's all educated guesswork. But I'd stake my worst guess against the best guess of anybody else in the business."

"If that's the best your competition can do, I'd say you don't have much to worry about."

"They're usually a lot more active over there. Don't know why it's so quiet today."

"Let's see your mine."

Hart's men were hustling to and fro, pushing wheelbarrows full of dirt, carrying timbers, making measurements. It seemed rather chaotic, but somehow they never got in each other's way.

"Here it is," Hart said, stopping in front of a hill. "This is the entrance to the mine."

The opening was humble, and almost lost in the morning sun shining brightly on the exposed dirt of the hill. It was little more than a hole in the ground, framed in rough timber. Inside was dark, though the air coming out of it seemed a little cooler than the outside air.

"Would you like to see inside? It's really not that deep."

"No," Sam said. "This is enough for me. I prefer the sunlight to the dark."

Bill Shannahan, Hart's foreman, stepped out of the mine entrance. He was smiling broadly, wiping dust off his face with a red bandanna.

"Thought I heard you two up here," he said. "You all missed a good show earlier this morning!"

"What show?" Sam asked, wondering if Malinda Melody was now giving mid-morning concerts in the streets of Jordanville.

"I'm surprised you haven't heard about it yet! Somebody took a couple of shots at Matt this morning from on top of Jordan's hotel. Well, Matt didn't take too kindly to this."

"I can imagine," Sam said, smiling slightly with a twinkle in his eye.

"Matt jumped off his horse, but not before spurring it right into the front door of the hotel, crashing through the porch! Then, quick as can be, he was up on that roof chasing his attacker."

"Did he get the rascal?"

"No, he was interrupted by a pretty woman. Somehow he got into Malinda's room and sweet-talked her into going out to dinner with him tonight. Doesn't that take all!"

"Like I said, no bets," Sam said, still smiling.

"It's all over town already," Shannahan said. "In the meantime, I've got to get back to work."

The foreman walked to a building several hundred feet from the mine entrance and waved Hart over. Sam took another glance at the mine opening, then joined Hart and Shannahan.

"Somebody's broken into our supply shed," Shannahan said, his good humor gone.

"Is anything missing?"

"Hard to say. They left a mess."

Sam calmly walked past the two men and entered the shed. His keen eyes scanned the upturned boxes, making mental note of their contents. He called out, "Hart?"

The miner stuck his head in the door.

"Have you done much blasting recently?"

"No. Why?"

"That box of explosives is only half full. I think maybe that explains what your thief was after."

Malinda Melody placed her shotgun against the wall, cocked her head to one side, and watched Jordan with a look as if to say, "I'm doing what I want to, and you can't stop me!"

Jordan remained calm. The only sign that he was upset was his chewing on his cigar. The room was quiet for long minutes after Matt Bodine and most of Jordan's other men had left Malinda Melody's room.

"Malinda," Jordan finally said. "I'm rather disappointed in you."

"So what if you don't like it? You hired me to be a singer, not your slave. You don't own me. If I want to have dinner with Mr. Bodine, that is my right."

"And you think I'd try to force you against your will? No, I'm too much of a gentleman for that, as you might say. I'm just rather disappointed that you took the side of a stranger, one who may very well be employed by my enemy."

"I don't care."

"The outcome of that fight may possibly influence the future of your career."

"Bull. You make enough money from the miners to pay my expenses and leave plenty for yourself. And I'm not fool enough to think that if you actually find gold out here that it will further my career."

"So your mind's made up? Very well. I would just recommend that you don't get too attached to Mr. Bodine." He gestured to Strep and the other men who remained in the room. "Come down to my office. We have business to discuss."

When he was once again behind his desk, and had poured himself a glass of whiskey, Jordan felt more in control.

"How much longer before we've cleared out most of our supplies from the mine site?" Jordan asked.

"Another few days, we figure," Strep said.

"That's too long. If we take too long, and move out too much, it'll give Hart some warning to clear out himself."

"What kind of loss are you willing to take?"

"I can take the hit a lot better than Hart. When you blow that dam and the water comes rushing down, destroying men and equipment and supplies, it'll ruin him. I've still got enough money to replace my losses. He doesn't."

"Still, if you lose too many men, it would be hard to replace them."

Jordan poured himself another glass of whiskey.

"You're right. But don't delay too long. Do it early in the morning," Jordan continued. "After most of Hart's men have started their work, but before they've really woken up. After that, Hart should be much more willing to negotiate. Start the rumor that work has slowed because we dug in the wrong place and we're moving operations. That way it won't raise too many suspicions."

"That still doesn't get rid of those two troublemakers," Strep said. "Even if you put a dent in Hart's operations, he's still got Bodine and Two-Wolves. I'm sure they're working for him, no matter what they say. I don't like either one of them, but I've come to especially dislike Matt Bodine. He had no right to be in Malinda's room. He should be shot."

"And you're the one to do it? You saw the way he outfought us and outdrew us. As fast as you are, you're not as good as Bodine. What we need is the very best. No matter the cost. Any ideas?"

"Money is no object?"

"Not to get rid of Matt Bodine and Sam Two-Wolves, and destroy Hart's organization."

"The very best gun I know about is a man named Phil Caphorn. He's rumored to have killed two dozen men in fair fights. I've personally seen him take down three men in one fight. Of course, that was five years ago. He may have slowed down some since then."

"What's he cost?"

"Last I heard he required $10,000 up front. The price would go up from there."

"Is he worth the price?"

"What's it worth to you to get rid of those two troublemakers and gaining a clear shot at Hart's land titles, without him being in the way to stop you? Aren't you talking millions?"

"Can you get hold of him?"

"He's based in Junction City. I could send a message to him. If he's interested, he could be here in a matter of days."

Jordan stood, walked over to a safe in the corner, opened it, and pulled out a bag of coins. He lifted it, enjoyed its weight, then tossed it to Strep.

"Get him. This is his $10,000. In gold. That should get his attention."

"I'll have my men get on this right away." Strep smiled. "That Matthew Bodine is dead meat."

"I still wouldn't count on making any time with Malinda, even with Bodine out of the way. You haven't made any progress that I can see."

"She doesn't think my manners are refined enough, though I can't see that stinking Bodine being any better than me. I think we ought to keep a watch on her."

Jordan shrugged. "To be honest, I'm not sure I care what happens to her. She's more valuable to me as a happy performer, and if having dinner with Bodine makes her happy, who am I to argue? If something were to happen to her that interfered with her performance duties, I'd probably think differently."

"I don't like her with Bodine."

"And if I were you, I'd watch that temper," Jordan said. "Up in her room, he almost killed you. I know you're sweet on Malinda, but so is every other man in Jordanville. Just be patient, and Bodine will get his just reward."

Shannahan stepped inside the supply shed with Hart and Sam.

"How much is missing?" Hart asked.

"This wasn't a full box, but it was about two-thirds full," Shannahan answered. His voice was measured. "Whoever took the explosives could do some damage, but their loss won't set us back any. We're a long ways from needing to do any major blasting." He

90

put the lid back on the box. "It still makes me mad. First that Parrish tries to make me out a fool in front of the whole town. Now somebody's stealing supplies."

"Parrish was taken care of," Sam pointed out.

"You beat him and saved my life, and I thank you for it," Shannahan continued. "But it's my own honor I'm thinking of. It's been grating at me ever since he first touched me with that bullwhip."

"Jordan said that Parrish is no longer working for him. He's probably not even in the area after the beating I gave him."

"No, he's still skulking around. I've caught glimpses of him. So have a few others. He's laying low. But if I catch him out in the open, I'll challenge him. See what he can do in a fair fight."

"Shannahan's an old boxer," Hart explained. "He's a tough fighter, but has this thing about honor."

"I can understand that," Sam said. "Sometimes a man's honor is his most important possession."

"Oh, I can fight like a brawler with the worst of them," Shannahan continued. "But it doesn't seem right to me."

"I understand that, too," Sam continued. "I learned to fight as an Indian, but in school I learned about boxing and other 'civilized' methods of fighting. There's a lot to be said for two men following agreed-upon rules to determine who is the better man, without actually killing each other."

"And I'm itching to show Parrish who's the better man."

"Why do I feel you've caught glimpses of Parrish because you've been looking for him?" Sam asked.

Shannahan smiled grimly in answer.

"Well, lock up this place as best you can," Hart said. "And keep your eyes and ears open. Jordan has plenty of explosives, so I doubt if he's behind this theft. It's probably just a lone prospector too broke to buy his own supplies. Even so, I have a feeling Jordan is going to try something pretty soon. You and Matt are shaking things up just being here. I can't see Jordan just standing around while you beat up his men and Matt steals his girl."

Jordan's comment was interrupted by a whistling. Matt rounded the corner, grinning like the cat that swallowed the canary.

"I heard you were in a little fight this morning," Hart said.

"But you somehow wound up getting the girl," Sam said.

"Haven't gotten her yet, but I will before

long," Matt said. "Women can't resist me."

"And he gets worse," Sam joked.

Hart rolled up his eyes as Shannahan smiled.

"Before you congratulate yourself too much, you need to listen to this," Sam said, more seriously. He explained the theft from the supply shed, about Parrish still remaining somewhere around town, and Hart's theory about the thief who took the explosives.

"I don't know if I agree with Hart about the thief, but I do agree that Jordan has something planned. He let me get away far too easily. I figured I'd have about six dead men on my hands before I got away from his bunch this morning. Instead, he just let me walk away. It doesn't seem in character for him."

"You going to go ahead and have dinner with Malinda?" Shannahan asked.

"Of course! It's not every day I get a chance to have dinner with a true vocal artist . . ."

Sam pulled Matt's hat down over his eyes and started to walk away.

"Like I said, he gets worse," Sam said. "Once he starts, there's no stopping him!"

"Good man!" Shannahan said.

CHAPTER EIGHT

Matt and Sam hoped for a quiet lunch, to get a little rest and talk over the situation in Jordanville. The town did not yet have a real restaurant, though it was filled with saloons. The two young men decided to try the little saloon where they had talked with Hart the previous night.

"Hey, Clancy!" Sam called out to the small, portly bartender. "You've got something in the way of food?"

Clancy smiled and yelled back, "Sure! It ain't fancy, but its filling!"

"Make it two of your specials and two beers!"

"Not much of a crowd today," Matt said.

"They're all working. They can't take time off from the job for lunch. The rush will be this evening."

Clancy brought the two beers and two dishes of stew on a tray. As he set the glasses down, he said to Matt, "I heard about your little escapade this morning at Jordan's hotel. You were running quite a risk, weren't you?"

"There'd be more risk in doing nothing. If you let somebody take potshots at you once, they'll try it again. I didn't catch the bastard, but he'll think twice before trying it again."

Clancy set the dishes on the table. "I'll say one thing about you boys. You sure know how to make enemies fast."

"It's a talent, that's for sure," Sam agreed.

"Rumor is you asked Malinda to dinner, right under Jordan's nose," Clancy continued. "And you lived to walk away!"

"That's pretty close to the truth," Matt said.

"Unbelievable! Eat up, boys. This meal's on the house. I'll bring you more beers in a few minutes."

Sam sampled the stew and exclaimed, "This is great!"

"It sure is!" Matt agreed. "Helluva lot better than your trail cooking!"

"Maybe if you did your share of the chores, you wouldn't have to eat so much of my cooking!"

"Aaah . . . you're still sore because I stuck you with clean-up duties this morning?"

"Maybe if you had stuck around a little

longer, you would've gotten in a lot less trouble," Sam suggested.

"And had a lot less fun!"

Sam finished off his stew. "All kidding aside, I don't like the situation in this town. Every day that passes brings Hart and Jordan that much closer to a shooting match. I temporarily pulled the fangs from Parrish, but he's still around and Jordan still has his other gunfighters. Hart is losing his patience. And with you pushing Jordan like you're doing, he's likely to lose his patience as well."

"Maybe it'd be better to get the fighting done sooner rather than later, when both sides might have lots of reinforcements," Matt said, thoughtfully. "I don't want anybody to get killed, but what if both sides were loaded up with top guns? It'd be slaughter on both sides. And who knows? Both sides may still be able to talk it out."

"Fat chance."

"Yeah. I'm afraid you're right." Matt called out to the bartender, "Hey, Clancy! We're ready for those beers!" When the bartender arrived at the table, Matt said, "The stew is great! How are you with other dishes? Say, maybe, fried chicken?"

"The chickens I can buy are scrawny, but I can make them juicy and tasty."

"Great! How about packing me a picnic lunch?"

Clancy winked. "It would be my pleasure! When would you like it to be ready?"

"Make it late this afternoon. I plan to have my picnic with Malinda before her show tonight!" Matt took another sip of beer. "You wouldn't happen to have any wine around here?"

"Only a few bottles of the homemade variety. But I made it myself!"

"Alright, throw in a bottle of that, as well," Matt said.

Sam just shook his head and took another drink of beer.

Malinda sat in front of the mirror for long minutes. Her eyes were open, but she wasn't watching the image in the glass. She was instead lost in her thoughts. It was early afternoon, long before she was scheduled to go on stage again, but she felt nervous.

She almost wished now that she hadn't agreed to have dinner with the cowboy who fell through the ceiling into her room that morning.

She picked up her brush and started to run it through her brown hair. She preferred to wear it loose, and it hung gently over her shoulders and the white cotton gown she was wearing.

Malinda had liked the cowboy — he had called himself Matt Bodine — in spite of the awkward way they met. She felt she was generally a good judge of character — her initial assessment of Nelson Jordan being the exception — and she had determined that Matt was not a dangerous man in the usual sense. He had the appearance of being tough if he needed to be, and the way he had faced down Jordan's men that morning had proven her right. Even more importantly, however, he had a sense of self-confidence that most men, even the ones that made their living with their guns, often lacked.

And he was also a gentleman! He had taken the awkward, even dangerous, situation he had found himself in and conducted himself with dignity and with manners. She had not been born with a silver spoon in her mouth, and had never been able to attend the Eastern finishing schools as other girls had, but she knew the difference between a man who was a gentleman and one who was not.

Nelson Jordan was not a gentleman in Malinda's eyes.

When she had first met him, Jordan had seemed a perfect gentleman. He was smooth and polished, well-educated, with money to burn. He had conducted himself honorably enough, and his promise to bring her West and let her sing was too irresistible to pass up. It hinted at elements of adventure as well as a chance to pursue a career that would probably be closed to her back East.

Except that when they arrived at this forsaken mining camp Jordan did not prove to be the gentleman that he seemed. He forced himself on her, ordered her around like a slave, made her perform in front of all the strange men every night.

She had fought back in her own way, and had managed to carve herself small amounts of personal freedom. She had kept it by presenting a tough façade, a haughty attitude that bordered on belligerence. She at times used her womanly wiles to keep her bodyguards — she thought of them more as wardens — also interested in her as a woman. But never before had she been so outright defiant as today, when she agreed to have dinner with Matt.

She knew she would have to pay for her defiance eventually, but in the meantime she was looking forward to dinner. Matt had seemed an interesting man. And Malinda thought that no matter what Jordan believed, she was still her own woman.

Malinda put down her brush, walked to the door and called out, "Jake! I want to go for a ride! Would you arrange it?"

But it was Strep that came to the door.

"Jordan thought you might want out for awhile," Strep lied. "So he appointed me your bodyguard again today. To make sure nothing happens to you."

Malinda said, "Let me get my shawl. You get the buckboard."

Strep tipped his hat.

"Right away, ma'am," he said.

Matt and Sam had spent almost two hours in Clancy's small saloon as various persons would stop by and talk. All seemed nervous. Like Matt and Sam, they felt something was going to happen, but didn't know what or when. Rumor had it that the Jordan mining operations had yielded disappointing results, which had forced work to slow. Some of the observers thought this might cause Jordan to increase the pressure on Hart to sign over his land. After hearing all the gossip, the blood brothers decided it was time to get some fresh air.

"You think it's safe for us to walk around in this town?" Sam asked, only half-joking.

"We've had it a lot worse in lots of other

towns," Matt reminded him.

"That is true," Sam agreed.

Still, they checked their Colts before stepping through the door into the street.

"I'm going to check out the hotel," Matt said suddenly.

"You must be crazy."

"I want to see if Jordan is repairing the damage to his building. He's a lawyer, you know, and may send me a bill for the repairs."

"You are crazy!" Sam said, but walked beside Matt down the street.

In spite of the uproar that morning, the actual damage to the building was minor. Jordan already had some craftsmen replacing the busted planks. Hammering on the roof indicated that similar work was taking place to patch the hole in the roof.

"Hope he uses better wood than before," Matt joked.

"Doubt if he plans to stay in this town long enough to care," Sam said. "Once he gets his mine working profitably, he'll probably sell for a handsome profit. He's not in it for the long run."

From around the corner of the building a buckboard came into sight.

"Don't look now, but it's your new girlfriend," Sam said.

"I see her. And that Strep fellow is with her."

"Don't do anything foolish."

"Do I ever do anything that's not careful and reasoned?"

"That's what I thought," Sam said. "I'll make sure the fight's fair."

"May not be a fight. I'm just going to say hi to Malinda."

"And I might as well be talking to a fence post."

"I think talking to a pretty girl is a lot better idea than talking to a fence post."

Strep was driving. When he spotted Matt and Sam, he started to look for a side street to turn on, but there was none in that section of town. So he tried to ignore the two blood brothers.

"Good afternoon, ma'am," Matt said, tipping his hat. "It's a nice day for a drive."

Malinda started to say something, but Strep popped the reins and the horse started at a faster pace. Strep had hoped to rush past Matt and Sam, but Matt had other ideas. As the vehicle passed him — almost running over his foot in the process — Matt casually leaped up on the buckboard and took hold of the reins.

"Like I said, good afternoon," he said, pulling on the reins to signal the horse to stop. "It's good to see you out and about. I was afraid after the problems this morning you might be a little hesitant."

"Yes, it is a nice day," Malinda said. "But I'm not worried about anything happening to me. I don't think anybody in this town would want to do me harm."

"Certainly not to a woman as pretty as you!"

Strep had tried to keep his temper under control, even after Matt had jumped on the buckboard. However, Matt and Malinda carrying on a conversation as if he wasn't even there angered Strep even more. He pushed against Matt, but it was like pushing against a brick wall. Matt refused to move.

"You flatter me," Malinda said.

"It's only the truth. Too bad you have such an ugly escort this pretty afternoon . . ."

The final insult was more than Strep could take. He stopped the horse, put on the brake, and leaped at Matt. Strep was a big man, and even though Matt had expected the move, he could no longer hold on to the vehicle. Both men landed on the hard ground, Strep on top. The breath was almost knocked out of Matt, which was made worse when Strep punched him twice in the gut as he lay on the ground.

Matt did not stay on the ground for long, however. With strong arms, he reached up and pushed against Strep's chest. Though Strep resisted, he still went flying backwards into the dirt.

Matt rolled and got his knees under him. Strep quickly regained his feet and jumped at the other man. Matt put his hands together and struck upwards with both fists, hitting Strep in the mouth as he landed. Though the blow landed hard, its only effect was to produce a small trickle of blood from the corner of his mouth.

Matt again fell backward with Strep on top, but this time he was better prepared. His blow to Strep's mouth had lessened the impact. Matt grabbed the gunfighter by the throat and pivoted, throwing him to the ground. He kept his grip, trying to cut off the other man's windpipe. Strep's neck was broad and muscular and Matt could not get the grip he was looking for. Strep managed to bend his knees and get his booted feet under Matt's stomach. He extended his legs, sending Matt over his head. The move was awkward, allowing Matt to land gently.

Strep quickly jumped to his feet and tried some quick punches to Matt's face, which were easily blocked.

Similar blows by Matt found their mark

more effectively. Matt worked on Strep's face, forcing his mouth to become even more bloody. In minutes, an eye also began to swell shut.

Under Matt's barrage of blows, Strep began to step backwards toward the hotel. The men working on the porch had taken a break to watch the fight, leaving their tools temporarily abandoned. Strep stepped on a hammer, causing him to lose his balance.

From his position on the ground, he reached out and grabbed a piece of splintered wood with one hand and the hammer in the other.

"Going to do a little carpentry work?" Matt asked. "Hope you're a better carpenter than you are a fighter."

Matt was a little winded himself, and was taunting Strep in the hope he would get even angrier and make a stupid mistake, which is what happened.

Strep struck out repeatedly with the wood, each time missing his opponent. Matt ducked and weaved, carefully timing Strep's swings. Before Strep could think of another line of attack, Matt rushed in under one of the swings, the rough wood barely creasing his broad shoulders. He managed to hit his shoulder solidly in Strep's stomach and followed up with a flurry of blows to the stomach and head.

Finally, the series of blows from Matt's rock-hard fists had their intended result. Strep finally became glassy-eyed and the board started to slip out of his hand. Matt caught the board in mid-air, slammed it once against the side of Strep's head, forcing him to the ground. He was not unconscious, though he remained perfectly still.

Matt tossed the board into Strep's lap.

"I hate being interrupted when I'm talking to a lady," Matt said.

"Next time I'll kill you," Strep said.

"You try it, and you'll be pushing up daisies." He turned to Malinda. "It's a little early yet, but would you like to go out to dinner anyway?"

"I'd be delighted!"

Matt got up on the buckboard seat beside Malinda.

"Let me change shirts and get our meal, and we'll be on our way!"

CHAPTER NINE

Jordan's men had ridden hard and fast over sometimes harsh terrain, almost killing three horses. It was worth the costs, however, since the men had made it to Junction City in record time. It was dark, but Phil Caphorn would be up late, as always, gambling in the Silver Lady Saloon that served as his informal office.

A tall man named Slim and a shorter man named Webb had been chosen to relay the message and the gold to the gunfighter. Neither of Jordan's men were particularly fast with a gun, but they were tough and they could be trusted. Fortunately for them, they had met no serious trouble along the way. Though they were dog-tired, the gold remained intact in the bag.

Neither Slim nor Webb were very familiar with larger cities, having lived most of their lives in the parts of Colorado that remained remote from civilization. The first thing that caught their eyes as they rode into Junction City was its sheer size. Compared to it, Jordanville was little more than a wide spot in the road.

It took an hour for the two to find their way to the Silver Lady Saloon. They received their second surprise when they walked into the Silver Lady.

Compared to Jordanville's establishments — even the Jordan Hotel — this business was nothing less than sumptuous. The glassware was shining, the felt on the card tables was fresh and unmarked, the girls wore bright, new-looking outfits. And almost every customer was dressed in clean, expensive-looking clothes. It made Jordan's men feel shabby and out of place. Still, they had a job to do.

Finding Phil Caphorn was relatively easy. He was seated with his back to a wall playing cards with five other well-dressed men. He was wearing a dark suit and double pearl-handled guns. The hair that stuck out from under a broad-brimmed, light-colored hat was jet-black and combed back. He had a thick, black mustache.

Jordan's men approached Caphorn quietly, but with a firm stride. Webb held the bag of gold.

For long minutes, Caphorn ignored the

two as he played out his hand.

"I see your $500, and raise you $700," he said calmly, forcing all but one of the other players to drop out, even though there was already a large stack of chips in the middle of the table.

Betting continued for a few more minutes.

"My ace-high straight flush beats your four-of-a-kind," he finally concluded, showing his hand.

He nonchalantly pulled his winnings toward him. Only then did he look up at Jordan's men.

"You must be Phil Caphorn?" Webb said.

"The penny-ante games are down the street," Caphorn said. "If you're looking to hire me, you couldn't afford my fee, even if I was interested in working. Which I'm not. I'm on vacation."

The others at the table laughed nervously.

"We're not here to play a game," Slim said. "We're here to talk business with you. Not for us, but for our boss."

And who might your boss be?"

"Nelson Jordan."

"Never heard of him." Caphorn gestured and said, "Deal the new hand."

Webb stepped closer to Caphorn and opened the bag so that only he could see its contents. "We're here to offer you cash money for your services," he said.

Caphorn looked into the bag, but his poker expression never changed.

"Let me finish this hand, then we'll talk," he said.

On that hand the gunfighter lost a little, though his gains still totalled far more than his losses for the night.

"Okay, boys," he told the other players. "That's it for me tonight. Come back tomorrow for another game."

The other men grumbled, but knew better than to argue with a well-known killer. They left the table. Slim and Webb took two of the vacated seats.

"So your boss knows my fee. I'd say you have more than enough in that bag to hire me. So what's the game?"

In few words, Jordan's men outlined the problem that their boss faced and the solution he hoped that Caphorn could bring to the problem.

"So it's just a matter of facing down some hired gun? No challenge there. I really don't need the money now. Why should I take the job?"

"The man our boss wants you to face is named Matthew Bodine. You know him?"

Caphorn looked thoughtful. "Now that's a different situation," he said. "Bodine is starting to make a name for himself. Killing him would be a nice feather in my cap, so to speak."

He waited, until Jordan's boys caught on and laughed politely.

"So, you'll take the job?"

"Hand over the gold, boys. Then you can ride home and tell your boss I'm on the job. I'll be riding in within the next few days. Tell him to have the rest of the gold ready."

"Rest of the gold?"

"My total fee for this job will be $25,000 even. Tell your boss that if he doesn't like it, I'll just keep riding. But this $10,000 is my retainer. Got it?"

Jordan's men nodded.

"Good. Now get out of here and let me get back to business."

Jordan's men didn't have to be told twice.

It took Matt less than five minutes to change shirts and pick up the picnic meal that Clancy had prepared for him and Malinda. The woman waited patiently in the buckboard and smiled when Matt returned. Matt picked up the reins and started down the road.

"Matt? You don't mind if I call you Matt?"

"Please do."

"Why were you so rough on Strep?"

"One reason is that I don't particularly like him. A more important reason is that I didn't much think he would leave us alone unless I proved to him it would be better for him to leave us alone. And it could have been worse for him."

"How?"

"He could have drawn on me."

"Strep's pretty fast. But I saw your moves this morning. You're right. If he had drawn on you, he'd be a dead man now. I'm glad you didn't have to kill him."

"You sweet on him?"

"That's a mighty personal question."

"Found out a long time ago the quickest way to find out something is to ask."

Malinda laughed. The buckboard was going slowly through the rutted streets toward the outskirts of town. Many of the workers and miners stopped to get a better look at Malinda. By now most of the town knew about Matt and her.

"No, I'm not sweet on Strep. I don't even particularly like him, though he wishes I did. I just hate to see anybody hurt."

"Seems to me then that your taste in men-friends is kind of strange."

"Jordan? He's not my man-friend. Oh, you might say we've been close in some ways. Closer than I would have wanted. But I owed him for giving me a chance to sing. When he said my opportunity would come out West, I never expected it to be in a place like this." She swept her hands to take in the town.

"But you like your life?"

Malinda sighed. Matt thought the way her body and head moved when she sighed made her look very pretty.

"I like singing. And parts of the West I like very much." The buckboard had now left the town and was starting to pass through the surrounding countryside. "I like the mountains. I like the grass and trees in the valleys. I like the country surrounding the town, like we're now passing through. I often have my bodyguard drive me out here, to help me relax and for inspiration." She paused and looked at Matt through half-closed eyelids. "How did you know I like it out here?"

"It was a gamble."

"I think you sometimes gamble an awful lot."

"It keeps life interesting. You said you don't care for Nelson Jordan?"

"I didn't say that. I used to care for him a lot. At first, I even liked the sense of adventure, of exploring someplace new and exciting. But I don't particularly care for the town. And I don't particularly care about working for Nelson Jordan anymore. He's too possessive. He acts like I'm just another of his business enterprises."

"Why don't you go elsewhere? You're good enough to in someplace civilized. Maybe Denver. Maybe even back East."

"I'm from the East. I've thought about going back, but to do so would mean leaving Jordan. And that's something he would never let happen." She put her hand on Matt's. "Where are we going?"

"There's a nice little clearing up ahead where my brother and I made camp last night. I thought it'd be a nice place for a picnic."

Malinda settled back on her seat, watching the trees and occasional flash of river through the trees.

"You're direct. So I'll be direct."

"Shoot."

"That man with you. Is he your brother?"

"Blood brother. We are bonded for life by the Cheyenne ritual. It makes us as close as if we were raised by the same family."

"What's in all this for you? I mean back in town. You've made enemies of Jordan. He thinks you're on Hart's side. What are you getting or hope to get out of this fight?"

"Not a thing."

"I don't think I heard you right."

"For some reasons I don't want to get into, Sam and I feel very strongly about certain things. One of them is fairness. We got involved initially because we wanted to even the odds a little. Now that we're involved, we are going to see it through. We never start something we can't finish."

"That's interesting."

The buckboard had now reached the clearing. Matt hollered "Whoa!" to the horse, set the brake, and climbed down from the buckboard. He held out his hand and helped Malinda to the ground. Matt then cleared a grassy spot near the river, placed a blanket for a tablecloth, then set out the dinner.

"It's rather simple, hope you don't mind," Matt said.

"And you brought wine! Don't be silly. It's wonderful! It's more than any man has done for me in a long time."

"That's hard to believe. Every man in this town adores you."

"That doesn't mean they understand what it takes to make a woman happy."

Matt poured each of them a glass of the homemade wine.

"Then let's toast," he said. "To your happiness!"

"And to yours."

They clinked the glasses together and took a drink. To Matt's surprise, the wine was smooth and tasty. He would have to compliment Clancy.

"And what would make you happy?" Matt asked. "To go home again, back East?"

Malinda sighed again. "My father didn't like my idea of singing. He'd rather I got married and settle down. You know, have kids and stay home and all that. Guess it wouldn't be so bad if I could find the right man."

"And for now?"

"For now I intend to enjoy the moment. Would you please pour me another glass of wine?"

Jack Parrish was part of the crowd that watched Matt beat Strep in the fight. He had heard the two men promise to kill each other when they next met.

It couldn't be working out any better if he had tried! He had made sure that there was plenty of dislike between Matt and Jordan. That Matt was now after Jordan's woman, one that Strep also hungered for, made it even better!

Now it was a matter of waiting for his opportunity.

After the fight, Strep continued to sit in the dirt for long minutes, waiting for his head to clear. He shook off any hands offering to help him up as he cursed under his breath. He finally stood, shook his head to finish clearing it, and dusted himself off.

"I'll be damned if he gets away with this." Strep muttered the words, although several of those in town heard him clearly. "I'll get him for this!"

As the crowd started to disperse, Parrish heard a shouted voice behind him.

"Hey you! Hey Parrish, you low-life snake! Come and fight me like a man!"

The gunfighter didn't have to look to know it was the voice of Bill Shannahan, the man he had attacked the day before in the river, only to be saved by Sam Two-Wolves. Parrish glanced behind him, saw that much of the crowd remained between him and the Irishman. Parrish wasn't scared of the other man, but he didn't want to be forced to deal with him at this time. So he slipped into the crowd, and then down an alley, to avoid a confrontation.

Maybe later if Shannahan wanted to fight, Parrish would oblige him. For now, however, he had other fish to fry.

CHAPTER TEN

To some of the people in town, Matt may have come across as a little crazy to go after Jordan's girlfriend. Sam, however, had known Matt all of their lives. They had grown up together, played together, fought together. Though they continually traded insulting banter, each knew how the other thought and respected each other's ideas. Sam knew that Matt's interest in Malinda was only partially the reason why he had walked into a fight with Strep. It was usually better to bring the battle to the other person than to let them bring it to you, which is what Matt was trying to do.

Tensions had been bottled up for too long. Something had to blow soon. And when it did, there might no controlling the results.

Yet something felt oddly wrong to Sam. It was only a vague feeling, one that most men would have simply shrugged off. But Sam had learned from experience to trust his instincts. He wasn't sure where following his hunches would take him, but it had to be better than taking no action at all.

It was nearing dusk. The streets were more crowded than earlier in the afternoon, but it was still a very small town and most of the activity was in or near the saloons. Sam wandered among the small crowds, then slipped down a side street toward Jordan's hotel. The workmen had finished their job and left, but it was the rear of the building that interested Sam.

As he expected, the ground near the building was torn up too badly to show any decent tracks. His trained eyes, however, noted the probable way that Matt's attacker had taken to the roof and then escaped when Matt fell through the rotten spot in the wood into Malinda's room. Again, on a hunch, Sam removed his boots, hid them carefully, then climbed onto the roof. He moved so quietly in his bare feet that nobody in the hotel would ever suspect he was above them.

The workmen had also repaired the hole in the roof. It would be surprising if they left anything behind. Still, Sam examined every square inch of the roof, just in case. His efforts yielded no success. Disappointed, Sam moved quietly back to the edge of the roof, and examined the street below.

How had Matt's attacker gotten away so quickly? He probably had his horse tied somewhere close. It would have to be someplace at least partially hidden, yet easily gotten to. Sam's eyes fixed on an area between two buildings a short distance from the hotel. It would be a matter of a few steps from the hotel roof to a horse waiting there.

Sam put his legs over the edge, dropped quietly to the ground, put his boots back on, and walked over to where the getaway horse must have been.

Though the ground seemed torn up beyond all hope, Sam's keen eyes noted partial impressions where the horse had waited impatiently. And very near the building was one well-shaped hoofprint. To most people it would mean nothing. To Sam, it was as unique as a fingerprint. He memorized its shape, its size, and the fact that the shoe was worn down.

It wasn't much, but Sam had tracked down other men with less than this to go on.

The sun was starting to go down. A cool breeze was blowing in from the river. Matt and Malinda took the final sips of the homemade wine.

"It's been wonderful," Malinda said. "I can't remember when I've had so much fun. But you know what they say: All good things must come to an end."

"I've never much believed that."

"No, Matt, I guess you wouldn't. You sure don't live your life that way."

"I know that someday there may be a bullet marked with my name, or a horse that's a tad too wild. But I'd rather take my chances and experience as much of life as possible while I can!"

"That's one of the qualities I find fascinating in you. But I need to get back to town and get ready for tonight's performance."

"What if I don't bring you back?"

"You'd have an awful lot of jealous miners after your hide! Why, you might be lucky to even get out of town alive!" She lowered her eyes and added softly, "Or so I've been told."

Matt laughed. "Very well, but I expect to see you again!"

"I'd be disappointed if you didn't."

Sam made his way back to Hart's supply shed. Though light was now getting scarce, there was still enough for Sam's keen eyes. The ground around the building was hard packed and did not take prints. Still, there were damp patches near water troughs and other areas where a print might be found. If he found another hoofprint to match the one he found near the hotel, he might be on to something.

He started just outside the door, where the lock had been broken, and moved outward, his eyes scanning the ground. He finally found what he had been looking for behind some bushes several feet from the path leading to the shed.

The print was only partial, but matched the earlier print.

Of course, in themselves the prints proved nothing. But it was something that might be useful at some later time. Sam had learned to always remember the details, for you never know when a piece of information would prove valuable.

Sam had been crouching close to the ground, to get a better look at the print. He stood, stretched, and felt a tingling in his back. He loosened the gun in his holster, stepped out from around the shed into the street. The setting sun cast long shadows on the street.

"I see you skulking around," a voice said. "Probably trying to figure a way to break into the building and steal something."

"Come on out in the open," Sam said, holding his empty hands in front of him. "If you have a beef with me, come on out and talk about it. I'm a reasonable man."

"I didn't like you the moment I saw you and your Indian friend."

"I think you have it backwards. My brother is not Indian. I am. Or half Indians. Maybe the proudest half."

"Makes no difference. Injun is injun."

Sam was a reasonable man, most of the time. But he had been pushed about as far as he could be pushed. And if there was one thing he couldn't stand it was racial slurs directed against him and his heritage.

"Come on out in the open."

A man holding an older model revolver stepped out into the long shadows of the street. He looked familiar, but Sam couldn't place him at first. Then he remembered. It was the man named Rex who had caused problems the night before at Jordan's saloon. Then he was drunk, which had perhaps blunted his hatred as well as his judgment. Sam and Matt had been able to avoid a shooting then.

Now Rex was sober, with anger and hatred in his eyes. The revolver in his hand was aimed at Sam's stomach.

Rex's talk was starting to draw a crowd.

"Indians aren't good for anybody or anything. Now you're after our women."

"Like I said, Matt Bodine is not Indian, though we are bonded together as blood brothers. And he isn't after your women. He is simply having a meal with a woman he admires, as do you."

Sam knew it was more hopeless to try and reason with a bigot than with a drunk. Still, he felt he had to make the attempt.

Somebody in the crowd called out, "Forget it, Rex. Go on home."

Rex acted as if he hadn't heard. He continued, "I'm going to kill me an Indian, and take that necklace around his neck as a souvenir . . ."

Rex's gun was cocked and aimed as he started to squeeze the trigger. Sam's gun was still in its holster. It was intended murder, and Sam had no choice but to defend himself.

He fell to the ground and rolled as he drew his gun. The bullet from Rex's revolver almost grazed his back as it hit the ground and raised a puff of dust where Sam had just been.

Sam fired a shot while still on the move. The gun belched flame and the slug hit the other man squarely in the chest. He staggered, tried to aim his gun again.

Sam fired twice more, spacing the shots within inches of each other.

Blood seeped through Rex's shirt and he fell lifeless to the ground.

Sam stood cautiously. This was clearly a case of self-defense. There was no law in this town, however, and the crowd might take Rex's position and try to get together a hanging party.

But nobody made a threatening move toward Sam. The excitement over, they went back to their pursuits as a couple of volunteers dragged the body from the street.

"It's not the first shooting we've seen in this town, and won't be the last," Hart said from behind Sam.

"It's such a waste," Sam said.

"True. But most of the shootings here have been in the back. At least you two faced each other. You may not be so lucky next time."

Matt and Malinda rode in relative silence back to town. It was not an uncomfortable silence. It was more the easy feeling two people get who are simply enjoying each other's company.

Finally, near the hotel, Matt said, "I still have a couple of questions for you."

"Yes? I've been waiting all night for the

question."

"Is Malinda Melody your real name?"

The woman laughed. "So *that's* the question! If you don't tell anybody, I'll tell you my real name."

"I won't tell a soul."

"Smith. My given name is Malinda Smith. Not very catchy, is it?"

"Sounds good to me. But the way I look at it, a name is what you make it. But you acted like you thought I was going to ask you another question. What would that be?"

"I thought you were going to ask if you could kiss me."

"That was my other question."

Matt got the answer to his second question as her lips met his.

He had just started to enjoy their soft and inviting warmth when he heard the gunshots.

"That's Sam," Matt said. "He may need my help."

"How do you know it's him?"

"It's just a feeling. We've been riding together long enough that it's almost a sixth sense."

"Then go. Here's the hotel. I'll be alright."

"I'll see you again?"

"Of course."

And then Matt was gone, disappearing

into the shadows to back up his brother, if needed.

Had anybody seen Matt and Malinda arrive back in town? Parrish doubted it. And if they had, who cared? She still would have been last seen with Bodine, so her disappearance would naturally be credited to him.

Parrish waited patiently by his horse, watching the buckboard drive up to the hotel. He was a little surprised that Strep or another bodyguard was not around to receive her. But maybe Jordan was miffed and didn't want Malinda to think he was upset by this turn of events?

Malinda and Matt's final kiss was cut short when the gunshots rang out. Malinda gave Matt a final quick peck on the cheek as he stepped down from the buckboard and ran toward the shots.

This was the chance that Parrish had been waiting for.

CHAPTER ELEVEN

Malinda was surprised at her reaction to the stranger in town. Matt Bodine surely wasn't any better or worse than any of the hundreds of other Western men wanting to meet her and know her . . . and more. She was not overly vain, but she knew that many men in Jordanville would kill for the chance at even the quick kiss she had given Matt.

And why had she warmed up to him so much? She first agreed to have dinner with Matt as a dig at Jordan, to show him that he still did not entirely own her. It was more a product of her stubborn streak than anything else. She hadn't expected to have a good time. And she certainly hadn't expected to tell him her life story.

On the other hand, Matt Bodine and his blood brother and partner, Sam Two-Wolves, seemed to be the kind of men to do the unexpected. Perhaps it was not unreasonable for the same to happen to those they came into contact with?

Malinda watched as Matt tipped his hat and took off in the direction of the gunshots. She watched until he turned the corner, and then disappeared from sight. Malinda realized that though she had talked a lot about herself, he had revealed little about his past. She wondered about where he had been, what he had seen, what his future plans might be. Malinda decided that if circumstances were different, she might even wind up liking Matt a lot . . .

She knew she should be getting ready for that night's show. Still, she sat in the buckboard, listening to the sounds of night. The natural sounds of insects and birds were almost drowned out by the noise spilling out of the saloons into the street. She heard footsteps in the dark alley, and figured it was Strep or another of Jordan's men. It would be just like Jordan to get impatient and send men out looking for her.

Malinda lifted the bottom of her dress slightly and started to step down from the buckboard when she suddenly felt strong arms around her body and a rough hand over her mouth.

She tried to bite the hand and then to scream. To her surprise, it was Matt's name at the tip of her tongue. It made no difference who she called for help, since the words were immediately choked off by a gag stuffed into her mouth.

The woman tried to kick and scream, but the hold on her was too tight. Her hands were quickly tied behind her and a bag slipped over her head and a blanket wrapped around her body. She felt herself lifted off the ground, carried a few dozen feet, and dumped on the back of a horse. She felt the rear of the saddle under her, and guessed that whoever was kidnapping her had placed her on the back of the horse he was riding. Malinda wriggled and kicked, but all she managed to do was fall off the horse to the ground.

The jolt knocked the wind out of her, and she couldn't scream now even if her mouth wasn't gagged.

Who was doing this to her? Could Jordan be going to extremes to punish her for having dinner with Bodine? Who else would *dare* to do this to her?

Her unseen attacker lifted her from the ground, but before she could make another move, the woman felt a quick, jarring blow to her head with what could have been the handle of a gun.

Malinda's questions came to a sliding halt as she lost consciousness.

■ ■ ■ ■

The crowd had already started to clear and Rex's body was being dragged away when Matt came upon the scene and quickly figured out what had happened. Sam, though appearing nonchalant, kept his eyes on the crowd in case anybody else wanted to make trouble.

"Same guy that gave us trouble last night," Matt said.

Sam nodded in agreement. "I wish these troublemakers would think a little before they start shooting," he said.

"They never have, and I guess they never will."

Sam's face suddenly broke into a grin. "Well, Mr. Ladies' Man, how did your dinner date work out?"

"I didn't make her sing for her supper, though I was tempted," Matt said. "I might have guessed that she was just another saloon floozy, with a little better voice than most. That wasn't the case. She really is a nice woman."

"Then what's she doing with you?"

Matt grinned back. The two men then started walking down the street, side by side.

"Anything new on this Jordan-Hart fight?"

"I may have a lead, but I can't be sure just yet. I do have a gut feeling that this thing will come to a head pretty soon. And you're not helping matters any by stirring the pot."

"It's more fun to keep things stirred up."

"Yeah. I know. What's your next step?"

"To see Malinda's show again tonight, of course."

"Of course. She give you some free tickets?"

"Nah. I wouldn't take advantage of a woman's favors to get me a free admission!"

Sam's response was a snort. "While you're at the show, I'm going to do a little more snooping. There's one trail I'm curious about."

"You're going to try to pick up a trail in the dark?"

"Why not? Sometimes starlight brings out features lost during the day."

"Have my horse saddled, and I'll join you after the show."

"You're so generous!"

"Guess I have a weak spot in my heart for you, brother."

"Or in your head!"

Parrish had made his camp a few miles down river. His trip out of town with his prisoner was uneventful. The few who saw him didn't suspect anything unusual. He hadn't made any special attempt to cover his tracks, since he figured he wouldn't be followed.

He chuckled to himself when he thought of the scene when Malinda didn't make her show. If he guessed correctly, Matt Bodine would be right in the middle of the crowd. He and Sam might beat one man, or even a gang of men. Surely they could not escape an entire town of enraged men.

Parrish glanced over at the woman, sitting at the edge of the light cast by the campfire. She was tied. The sack had been removed while the woman was still unconscious and replaced with a blindfold. The gunfighter figured the woman was a little bruised, but otherwise unhurt.

"You want some coffee?" he asked.

Malinda said stiffly, "How can I drink it with my hands tied?"

"I can help you."

"I'd rather die of thirst."

"Suit yourself."

Parrish kicked another stick onto the fire and took a closer look at the woman. She was prettier than most women and she had a certain amount of class. Still, Parrish wasn't sure what all the hoopla was about.

One woman was about like any other woman in his mind.

Parrish wondered what he would do with the woman when he was through with her. He could let her go, since she couldn't identify him. He supposed he could ransom her back to Jordan. Or it might be better revenge on Jordan for the woman to simply disappear.

He would make that decision later. For now, he wanted to see the show in town that would take the place of the absent Malinda Melody.

The gunfighter kicked some dirt on the fire, tossed a blanket over Malinda to protect her from the evening dampness, and mounted his horse for the ride into town.

Matthew Bodine knew he had been pushing his luck. Some of the men in town would be jealous of his moves on Malinda. Jordan might be looking for some way to even the score. Rex's friends might be looking for revenge. It was not in Matt's nature to "play it safe" and blend into the background, but he did know the value of caution. So he waited until Malinda's show was about ready to start and then situated himself near an exit.

It had only been a little more than twenty-four hours since Matt and Sam had entered Jordanville, but now everybody knew them. Many in the crowd cast sidelong glances at Matt. Other small groups talked in whispers among themselves. All gave him a wide berth.

As showtime neared, the men grabbed their drinks and moved as close to the stage as possible, jostling each other for standing room only. The crowd grew silent in anticipation.

Only this time Malinda did not appear onstage.

The men stared in amazement. Slowly, whispers started in one corner of the room and spread to the others.

Five minutes passed. Then ten minutes passed. After twenty minutes the crowd was restless. The room seemed even more hot and crowded than usual.

Nelson Jordan stepped on stage. He was greeted with a chorus of boos and catcalls.

"Gentlemen, there's been a slight delay," he said.

A voice in the crowd called out, "Where's Malinda?"

Another voice cried, "Get off the stage! We want Malinda! We paid our money! We want Malinda!"

Jordan held out his hands and said, "Give

us a few more minutes. If the show must be canceled tonight, we will refund your money!"

"We don't want our money! We want Malinda!"

Jordan disappeared from the stage.

Matt frowned. What had happened to Malinda? He had left her at the hotel in plenty of time to make the show. When he had left her, she was in fine shape. So why wasn't she onstage?

Matt decided he had better look into the matter. He edged toward the door and was almost there when Nelson Jordan stepped between him and the door. Matt stopped with his face just inches from Jordan's.

"Why isn't Malinda onstage?" Matt asked in a soft voice. "If you've hurt her in any way because she had dinner with me, I'll kill you with my bare hands."

"I have the same question of you," Jordan said in an equally soft voice.

Sam wasn't sure what he was looking for. He just had a gut instinct that if he kept looking, something would jump out at him.

He covered the main roads leading into town, and a few smaller paths. In most places, of course, the ground had been trampled into dust. Even so, there were enough isolated prints that Sam could piece together information.

Finally, along one of the lesser-traveled paths, he found something interesting: a hoofprint that matched the ones he had seen in town. This time it was much deeper in the soft dust, as if the horse had carried a heavier load than usual.

Sam thought it would be interesting to see where this particular trail led.

He remounted his horse and took it at a run back into town to get Matt's horse ready for him. Sam thought this was one hunt that Matt would want to participate in.

Matt didn't like the odds. Jordan was between him and the door. Behind him was a room full of angry miners. And Malinda was missing.

"You were the last person she was with," Jordan said softly. He was holding his cigar in his hand. "We found the buckboard, but the woman wasn't on it. As far as I know she never made it to the hotel. Just what is your game, anyway?"

"I was about to ask you the same thing," Matt answered. "I wouldn't put it past you to try and pull a dirty trick like this. Trying to frame me and maybe get a lynch mob after me."

Behind Matt, the crowd started to murmur. Matt heard his name mentioned several times in voices that got increasingly louder.

"Look at it from my viewpoint," Jordan said, reasonably. "You and your partner come into town uninvited. You beat up and shoot my men. You destroy my property. What makes me think you'd be beyond kidnapping?"

"Those were all fair fights," Matt said.

Matt could feel the crowd around him moving in closer.

Jordan said loudly, "You were the last man to see Malinda this afternoon. Obviously you did something to her. Perhaps you even killed her."

Matt lunged at Jordan. "That's a lie, and I'll see you in hell before . . ."

Strong arms pulled Matt away from Jordan. The lapels of the businessman's coat tore away in Matt's hands as another man tried to pin his arms. Matt didn't like to fight in such close quarters, but he had no choice.

He lifted a knee into the groin of the attacker in front of him and backhanded the attacker beside him. The man trying to hold him lost his grip. Matt whirled around and punched him in the stomach.

Several more of Jordan's men had stepped between Matt and the door. Several had pulled their guns, but did not use them for fear of hitting each other.

Matt didn't have that worry.

He pulled his Colt and fired three quick shots just over the heads of the men in front of him. In the crowded room, the gun sounded like cannon shots. The bullets cut through the hats and grazed the scalps of the men, sending them to the floor. There wasn't enough room for all of them, and they quickly got tangled up in each other's legs.

Matt stepped on the back of the closest man, jumped to the chest of the next one, and then leaped toward the window.

"Shoot him!" Jordan cried. "What are you waiting for? Shoot him!"

Several more shots exploded in the room. Matt heard one of the bullets as it whizzed past his head, missing him by only inches.

Matt rolled as he hit the ground. He looked around for the best escape route when he heard the sound of familiar hoofbeats.

Sam was racing his horse down the street, with Matt's reins in his hand.

"How'd you know I'd need you about this

time?" Matt asked as Sam tossed him the reins.

"I didn't. You just got lucky."

"You call this lucky?

"You asked for it."

"Yeah, I guess I did."

In seconds Matt was on horseback.

The angry miners had now gotten off the floor and were trying to climb through the window after Matt. Jordan's men fired more shots over their heads, sending the men in front to the ground once again.

"Come with me," Sam said. "I've got something to show you."

"As if I have a choice, with that angry mob behind me?" Matt asked.

By the time Jordan's men made it out of the building, the two blood brothers had already disappeared into the night.

CHAPTER TWELVE

Strep was still aching from the beating he had gotten earlier in the day. He was stiff and sore and irritable.

"To hell with Bodine, to hell with Malinda," he muttered between drinks of whiskey. "Any woman's a damned sight more trouble than she's worth."

When the others had stampeded out of the saloon after Bodine, Strep had remained standing against the bar. The building was now vacant except for him. He reached over the bar, grabbed the bottle and poured another shot.

As he drank, he looked out the window. The damned idiots were mounting horses to give chase. Not that it would do them any good, Strep thought. They'd make so much noise and get in each other's way so much that they wouldn't have a chance in hell of finding Bodine, Two-Wolves, or the woman.

If Bodine had the woman. As much as Strep hated Bodine and Two-Wolves, he wasn't sure they were the kind of men who would kidnap a woman. And if they were, they'd more than likely be a little more careful about showing their faces around town.

Outside, Jordan was waving his arms, giving orders. Strep noticed now that several more persons had joined the outer fringes of the crowd. They were Hart's men, perhaps curious about what was going on. Or maybe they had a hand in Malinda's disappearance? Some wore guns around their waists. A few carried rifles.

Tensions were already running high. Strep thought, *Wouldn't it be damned funny if the actual shooting started over a missing woman?*

Strep filled his glass again and took it to the door to better hear what was going on.

"I never thought you'd stoop so low as this," Jordan said. "We both know I'd win eventually. It was only a matter of time. So you had your men strike where you thought I'd be most vulnerable."

Hart stood with his arms crossed, a defiant look in his eyes. "I've had nothing to do with any of this," Hart answered. "And Heaven help me if I even thought of hurting a single hair of a woman."

"Well, she's missing."

"So she is. Maybe she just decided she's had enough of you and moved on. Did you ever think of that?"

Jordan inhaled cigar smoke, blew it out through his nose.

"I think you're getting desperate, and was somehow involved. I hold you personally responsible. If you don't produce her by morning, I'll come after you personally. I'm tired of playing nice."

"Bring all the thugs you want. We'll still beat you."

Jordan turned on his heel and headed back for the saloon. Strep moved out of his way as he entered.

"Why aren't you out looking for Malinda, too?" Jordan snapped.

"There's no chance that group of idiots could find anything. I'm going out on my own."

"Then do it," Jordan said.

Strep finished his glass of whiskey, then went outside to get his horse.

Parrish chuckled to himself as he watched Hart and Jordan almost come to blows. He had thought that the shooting might start tonight. Well, there was still the explosives he had stolen from Hart. That would surely be what it would take to finally get the two groups to start shooting at each other in a full-fledged war.

The gunfighter was stretched out in the hayloft of an outbuilding near the center of town. He couldn't hear all the words being said, but he could follow the action.

The two groups started to break up. Hart and several of his men headed toward the livery. Parrish pushed himself farther back into the shadows of the loft.

"You still looking for Parrish?" Hart asked.

"He's still around, somewhere," Shannahan said. "I heard some talk that he was spotted this afternoon headed out of town. I'll find him sooner or later."

"Make sure you find him before he finds you."

Parrish had heard enough threats from Shannahan. The gunfighter decided to take care of him right away. The shooting could always be blamed on an overzealous Jordan hand.

Parrish took aim, then stopped as Strep came out into the street. He looked up and down the street and then lit a cigarette.

Parrish let his gun down. If he shot now, Jordan's man would investigate and Parrish wasn't ready to let his whereabouts be known. There could be some awkward questions that he didn't want to get into now.

Hart and his men continued down the street. Strep waited until they had passed and then came over to the livery. Parrish heard the other man below saddle his horse and then ride out of the building.

With most of Jordan's men out chasing shadows trying to find Malinda, Parrish would now have a free hand to set the explosives.

Matt and Sam weren't too worried about the makeshift posse on their trail. Even though they seemed to be in a difficult situation, they didn't panic or go off half-cocked. They had succeeded against greater odds in the past, and knew they would again. After they got safely out of town, they took the opportunity to get a few hours' sleep in a cold camp. They were up before dawn, refreshed and ready to face the day.

The area where they had camped was well-secluded. Since they traveled light, it took only minutes to break camp. They warily circled around. Apparently their pursuers the night before had given up, for there was no sign of unusual activity around Jordanville.

Sam dismounted, followed by Matt.

Sam cast his eyes to the ground, started

walking slowly.

"This is not a well-used path," Sam explained. "With any luck, it should still be . . . Aha! Here it is."

Matt bent down to also examine the hoofprint.

"What good is one print out of all the hundreds of horses in this town?" Matt asked.

"I've found the same print in other parts of town where some of the mischief has been going on. By Jordan's hotel after somebody took a shot at you. By Hart's supply shed after it had been broken into."

"Good work, brother. Guess some of my talents are rubbing off on you!"

Sam got back on his horse.

"I'll admit you're a decent tracker, though not in my league," Sam said. "After all, we both learned from the same source. You take that side of the road, and I'll take this one. That'll give us a better chance to follow the trail."

It was not good ground to track on. It was mainly rocks, and what soil there was had been burned into a bricklike surface or stomped into powder. Even so, there was enough sign that trained trackers like Matt and Sam could follow.

The trail led away from town along the

path for about a mile. The rider they were following then had turned off the path to the left. The ground here was slightly hilly, with a little more grass. The sign here was a little easier to follow.

After another hour had passed, Sam held up his hand to stop. With silent hand gestures, Sam indicated that the camp of the man they were looking for was just a little ahead. Both men got off their horses, tied them to trees, and approached on foot. Matt took the left, Sam took the right.

They approached slowly, unsure how many men might be in the camp or where guards could be stationed. Matt was a little surprised that he found no indication of guards being posted. And the camp itself seemed deserted. Maybe it was just one man they were following?

Matt crawled closer to the small clearing, carefully pushed aside some brush to get a better look.

Sure enough, there was no sign of activity. Whoever had been in camp had left hours before.

A slight movement caught his eye. Somebody seemed to be under a blanket near the edge of the clearing.

Matt slipped back into the brush, circled around to come up to the tree from behind.

He moved to within a few feet of the figure, when it moved again and the blanket fell away to reveal a fair arm that was familiar to Matt.

Strep was admittedly not a great tracker, but he did know the area around Jordanville. His procedure for looking for Malinda was simple. He would start hitting all the possible sites around the area where the woman might be hidden . . . or buried.

He had been searching for most of the night. So far, he had no luck at all.

And then he got lucky.

He had paused briefly on a tall, rocky overlook. He looked out over the area, trying to determine where he would look next, when he saw two smaller figures below him.

It was a one-in-a-million chance that he had spotted Matt and Sam. He figured that they knew their way around the wilderness better than most, and would not be seen if they didn't want to be seen.

If those two were behind Malinda's disappearance, they would lead him straight to her. The trick now would be to follow without alerting them to his presence.

Again, luck was with him.

Strep had kept to the high ground, satisfying himself with a brief glance from time to time through the trees. Then, before more than an hour had passed, Matt and Sam were in the camp.

Strep hurried down the hillside.

If luck remained on his side, he could get the drop on them and rescue Malinda.

Matt cocked his gun, stood, and stepped into the clearing.

Still no movement occurred in or around the camp.

Matt walked around the campsite, scanning the brush around it, wanting to be sure that nobody remained in hiding and this was not some kind of trap.

"It looks clean," Matt said.

"Same here," Sam said, also stepping into the clearing.

Matt stepped over to Malinda as Sam kept a wary eye on the surrounding area.

"Good to see you again," Matt said, cutting loose the blindfold.

Malinda's eyes widened in surprise and delight. Matt's hand started to loosen the gag when he heard a noise in the brush and Sam again motioned for silence. Before Matt could comply another voice was heard.

"I thought that if I followed you, you'd lead me to the woman," Strep said. He stepped into the clearing, his gun in his hand and aimed straight at Matt.

"How'd you find us?" Matt asked, looking at Sam. "I didn't think we left a trail that *you* could follow."

"Keep your insults to yourself," Strep said. "You're not going to rile me this time. I'll admit I had some luck finding you. I just started checking areas around town that might be a campsite. I didn't know about this one, but I'll take good luck any day of the week."

"Before you shoot, don't forget that there are two of us, and one of you," Matt said. "And we're both faster than you."

"Killing you would be enough for me," Strep said. "And who knows? I might get lucky and get your partner, too, before I die."

"Would it make a difference if we could prove we didn't have a hand in kidnapping Malinda?"

"How do you propose to do that? I followed you straight to this camp. I caught you red-handed here with the woman. That's enough for anybody."

Sam motioned to the woman, who was now struggling against her bonds.

"Why don't you ask her," Sam suggested.

Strep motioned with his free hand. "Alright. Bodine, you untie her. But don't try any fancy stuff."

"The thought never even crossed my mind," Matt said.

As soon as the gag fell from her mouth, Malinda cried out, "Matt! I'm so glad to see you!"

"I kind of hoped our next meeting would be under slightly different circumstances," Matt joked.

Strep interrupted the two. "Malinda. Who kidnapped you?"

"I don't know. He got me from behind. He knocked me out and kept me blind-folded."

"Was it Bodine?"

"No, it was not Matt." Malinda's voice was so sharp-edged it could have cut steel.

"How do you know? You said you didn't see who it was. Bodine might be playing you along."

Matt finished untying her ropes. She rubbed her hands together to get some circulation back in them.

"I'm a woman. I would know Matt's touch anywhere."

Strep knew when he was beat. He hol-stered his gun again. Matt helped Malinda up from the ground. He examined the bruises on her face.

"I sure would like to find out who did this

to you," he said.

Sam started poking around in a bag near the center of the camp. He reached in, pulled out a whip.

"I think this might be the answer to your question," he said.

Strep looked at the two blood brothers and the woman.

"I'll ride into town with you all," Strep said. "But don't get me wrong, this doesn't mean we're friends. If I get a chance, I still plan to kill both of you. I'm riding into town with you because I don't want some mob to take that satisfaction away from me."

"You've got a big heart," Matt said.

"Like I said, keep your insults to yourself. I still don't trust you, and I want to make sure that Malinda gets safely back to town."

"Alright," Matt agreed. "A temporary truce. For Malinda's sake." He turned to the woman. "We don't have a buckboard or a wagon. Think you could ride with me, just this once?"

"I'd be happy to," Malinda said, taking Matt's hand and jumping up into the saddle behind him.

CHAPTER THIRTEEN

Phil Caphorn didn't expect much from Jordanville, and he wasn't disappointed.

He glanced with contempt at the sign on the outskirts of town with "Silver Creek" crossed out and "Jordanville" painted in. He laughed at the meager mining operations that had been started. He sneered at the ramshackle buildings, including the Jordan Hotel.

"Jordan this and Jordan that," he muttered. "Why would he even want to lay claim to a dip in the road like this?"

Caphorn had been born to a life of luxury, so had spent little time among the dirt and grit of those less fortunate. Early in his life he found he had a way with guns, which he quickly capitalized on. The money came fast and easy, financing his expensive lifestyle on a pile of bodies. Only once or twice had anybody even come close to matching him draw-for-draw, so he had developed a cocky attitude that matched his expensive habits. He wrinkled his nose at this poor excuse for a town as he rode down the one main street.

Apparently he had ridden into town in the middle of some local excitement, for many of the miners were running back and forth, yelling to each other and generally behaving like oafs. He threaded his way through the people, pausing in front of the Jordan Hotel to survey his surroundings before dismounting.

Caphorn knew from experience that this was probably the best this little town had to offer. If it weren't for the need to replenish his bank account (which happened with far too much regularity), he would never venture forth into these dirty little Western towns. Unfortunately, this was where his type of help was needed. It never ceased to amaze him how various parties in such poor areas could find the money to pay his fees. This town, for example, didn't look as if all the citizens combined could put together enough for a good dinner. Yet, Nelson Jordan had sent Caphorn his advance fee — and more. So like it or not, this ramshackle building would have to be his home for the next few days, at least until he could collect the remainder of his fee.

A few of those running back and forth cast

a curious glance toward him. Most of the people ignored him. Well, Caphorn hadn't expected a brass band, but he thought that some of Jordan's people would have at least been looking for him.

He tied his horse to a post, then entered the saloon part of the building. Slim and Webb, Jordan's men who had initially met with Caphorn, were at the bar, talking to a third man. Slim snapped to attention when he saw Caphorn, gestured. The third man stepped forward.

"My name's Grant Smith. You Phil Caphorn?"

"The same."

"Jordan's been expecting you. I'll go let him know you're here."

The gunfighter stepped up to the bar. He noted the stage on the far side of the room, now vacant. He said, "I want a whiskey." When the bartender didn't move fast enough, he said in a colder tone, "I want my whiskey *now.*"

Something in his voice made the bartender quickly put the bottle in from of him and move away without waiting for payment. Caphorn smiled, reached behind the bar for a glass, and moved to a vacant table near the stage.

Caphorn was on his second glass when

Jordan finally entered the room and approached the table. The gunfighter didn't stand or extend his hand in greeting. Instead, he took another sip of whiskey. Jordan sat down and gestured for his own bottle.

"During my stay here, this will be my table," Caphorn said. "I expect all my expenses and creature comforts will be met, in addition to my fees for the job."

"You don't waste words, do you?" Jordan said.

"Why waste words? Money is the language that speaks the loudest. Gold and silver always demand the greatest attention. You got my attention. What's the job you need for me to do?"

"I've got a problem here. No, I've got several problems. I've been trying to . . . negotiate . . . a deal for some land with one Clarence Hart. These talks were in the process of breaking down when two busybodies moved in. They haven't officially taken Hart's side, but they've been making mince meat of my men. I want them taken care of, either before the shooting starts or during."

"You're pretty sure the shooting will start?"

"Positive."

"Who are the men I'm going to kill for you?"

"They're partners, riding together. Matt Bodine. Sam Two-Wolves."

Caphorn had started to hear a few stories about the two men, but hadn't paid much attention to them. To him, they were just two more names on a list of potential rivals. Now, they were two more names on a list of dead men.

"Got my fee?"

"Name it."

"Twenty-five thousand. In gold. Up front."

If the figure shocked Jordan, he didn't show it. He continued to sip his drink.

"Alright. I'll have it to you before the day is over."

"No. I want it delivered to my bank in Junction City."

"But that could take at least another day!"

"I have the time to kill. Do you?"

"Alright. I'll have my men get on it."

Caphorn leaned back in his chair. "When's showtime?"

"Hell if I know."

The gunfighter gave Jordan a withering glance.

"It's your joint."

"My singer's missing. Last I saw her, she

was off on some damned outing with Bo-dine."

Caphorn laughed.

The uneasy truce was holding. At least for the first few miles, Matt, Sam, Strep, and Malinda rode in silence that if not comfortable, at least was tolerable.

Sam made a brief attempt at diplomacy.

"Maybe it was dumb luck that you found us," Sam said. "It was still better than those idiots in town could have done."

"I'm surprised you're not trying to goad me, like your friend's been trying to do."

"Naw, I'm not a rival for the object of his romantic affections," Sam said.

"Huh?"

"Matt thinks you're sweet on me, and that I might return the affection," Malinda explained.

"Hell, Malinda, you know I've never made a secret that I'm fond of you. But so is every other man in town."

"But they don't get to spend time with her," Sam continued. "It doesn't take a genius to figure it out. Although in Matt's case, he has such a thick skull that I wonder how it came to him . . ."

"Thick skull! Why, if it weren't for my brains, and my brilliant plan . . ."

"Nonexistent plan."

"No matter . . ."

The banter suddenly came to a serious halt when the whine of a bullet echoed around the small party. Almost instantly, Sam had placed his horse between him and the unseen gunman, Matt had pulled Malinda to a protective rock outcropping, and Strep had found similar protection. As if the first shot was a signal, the air was filled with the sound of bullets being fired. Most of them seemed to come from a hill a little ways up the trail.

"What's that about planning ahead?" Matt called out.

"Could have happened to anybody," Sam called back. "I figured these guys would have gotten tired and retired to their beds by now."

A shell bounced off a rock near Matt's head.

"Wrong."

Strep said, "What do these clowns think they're doing? We have Malinda. Shooting like this could kill her as well as you all. Let me do the talking."

"Be our guest."

"Hey! On the hill! Stop shooting! This is Strep!"

The shots slowed some, but still came in

rapid succession.

"Will you stop your shooting!"

A voice finally called out and the shooting slowed in bits and spurts, and finally stopped.

"Strep! Are you alright?"

"I've got Malinda here! Stop your shooting!"

"Taking credit for saving her, Strep?" Matt asked in a conversational tone of voice.

"Be quiet at least once, Bodine."

"I have a big heart. Go ahead and take credit. It may raise you a notch or two in town."

Another voice on the hill called out, "Strep! We know they're making you say that!" The comment was followed by a shot.

"Don't worry, Strep! We'll come and get you and Malinda!"

And suddenly the shots were as rapid and numerous as before. Matt, his good humor gone under the senseless attack, listened carefully to the pattern of shots being fired. The men weren't working as a team nor did they have any kind of organization. Matt waited for a break in the shots, then reached out from behind the rock and fired three shots in a fairly close pattern. A pained yell and a thump of a falling body indicated that Matt's educated guess had paid off.

"We could wait these guys out," Sam said. "But I have better things to do with my time. I'm going to circle around and see if I can't knock some sense into them."

"I'm not going to shoot against my own people," Strep said. "But I won't shoot you or Matt in the back. I owe you that for helping find Malinda."

"You've done the best you could."

"Don't forget I still may face you two down a little later. One of you may get killed."

"Or you." Sam's words were matter-of-fact as he slipped into the brush.

Strep looked in disbelief at Matt.

"Does he really think he can sneak up on them?" Strep asked.

"If Sam wanted, he could sneak into the President's dinner party for coffee and cigars," Matt said with a straight face.

Another bullet whizzed by his head. Matt returned the fire, to provide some cover for Sam.

Sam had learned tracking and fighting under some of the very best Cheyenne warriors. Matt had also learned many of the tricks, but had not mastered them as well as Sam. Sam moved quietly through the brush, barely moving a blade of grass or a leaf of a sapling. The rocks and soil had been warmed by the sun, but were not uncomfortable to the Indian warrior. As he moved, he thought of the days of his youth, when he would go on hunting trips with the older members of his tribe, and felt at one with his many ancestors who hunted buffalo and men in just this way.

In minutes, Sam was situated across a small hollow from one of the attackers. He was positioned by himself, shooting at Matt and the others down the hill. Sam, perhaps in the same spirit that his ancestors counted coup, stood silently until he was at his full height in front of the attacker. He could have killed the other man easily, but preferred to give him a more even chance.

His shadow fell across the other man, who turned his head in surprise. His eyes grew wide. His mouth fell open. No words came out. He had his rifle cocked, and started to pivot it toward Sam.

Sam raised his revolver and shot once. The bullet caught the other man in the chest. He clutched at the pain in his chest, but did not drop the rifle. He tried to raise it again for another shot. Sam shot first. The second bullet hit the other man within inches of the first bullet. The combined force of the two slugs forced the attacker backwards. He fell, dropped the rifle, and rolled down the hill.

It had all taken only a few seconds. A few of Jordan's men spotted Sam, but he again dropped to the ground and blended with the underbrush before the others could react.

The attackers were less confident now. They were not sure what had just happened. One made the mistake of lifting his head out from behind his hiding place, and had his hat removed courtesy of a shot from Matt's gun.

Sam had now moved to a location behind a spot where two men had situated themselves to get clear shots at Matt and the others. Sam called out, "I'll give you all a chance to give up. Stop your shooting, throw down your guns, and nobody else will get hurt."

"Keep your threats to yourself . . ." one of the two started to say, when he realized that the voice was *behind* him. He turned, said, "What the hell! I thought you were . . ."

He didn't finish his sentence, because he made the mistake of shooting at the voice. Sam pumped two quick slugs into him. His partner managed to actually snap off a quick shot in Sam's general direction, though they remained wide of their mark.

Without pausing for a second, Sam continued to fire, and pumped two more slugs into the second man.

They slumped against each other in lifeless poses.

Sam slipped behind a tree and called out, "Are you ready to give up now?" The shooting had now stopped. Sam continued, "Step out in the open. Throw down your guns. And you'll live. You heard Strep. We have the woman, and she's not harmed."

Slowly, Jordan's men stepped out in the open, placed their guns on the ground. Sam then also stepped into the open, where Matt could see him.

"We're coming up!" Matt yelled.

In minutes, Matt, Strep, and Malinda were riding up the hill, leading Sam's horse.

"What do you think?" Sam asked. "I promised we wouldn't kill them."

"Too bad," Matt said.

"We could tie them up and bring them back into town," Sam suggested.

"It is an idea."

"But I think they learned their lesson. If they walk back into town, maybe next time they'll think twice before shooting."

"You're too easy on them," Matt said.

"I also have a big heart," Sam said.

But he kicked the guns down the hill

before he mounted his horse and joined the others for the remainder of the ride back into town.

Caphorn's laughter still grated on Jordan's ears when he heard a more pleasant refrain coming from the street.

"It's Malinda! They found Malinda!"

"Well, Caphorn, we may have our regularly scheduled show tonight, after all."

Caphorn stood and followed Jordan to the street.

Jordan almost choked on his cigar when he saw Malinda riding behind Matt, with Strep and Sam riding on either side of them. When they got to the hotel, Malinda slid off the saddle. Jordan said, "What's this, Strep? What's going on?"

"I found Malinda. So did these two. They didn't have anything to do with her kidnapping."

Jordan glared at him.

"Are you a traitor? Have you turned against me?"

"When you hired me, you hired my loyalty. But in the interests of the woman, I went along with a temporary truce. If more of your men had gone along with it, there'd be more coming back alive."

Caphorn laughed again, as if he found the

situation funny.

Matt started to step out of the saddle, when something in Caphorn's voice caused him to pause. He froze, then repositioned himself. His hand was within easy reach of his gun.

He said quietly, "Phil Caphorn. So we meet again."

The gunfighter stopped laughing. He looked Matt in the eye. His hand was also near his gun.

CHAPTER FOURTEEN

Phil Caphorn was no longer laughing.

The gunfighter coolly looked Matt up and down, then at Sam, on the horse beside him, and finally at the small crowd that had gathered in the street, including Hart and some of his men.

"You don't look familiar," Caphorn finally said to Matt. "I don't recall ever seeing you before."

"You wouldn't," Matt replied. "It was years ago, when I was riding shotgun for a freight company. In a small town called Stone Butte. You faced down a young guy, no more than a kid. You killed him in cold blood."

Caphorn didn't remember the specific incident Matt referred to; there had been too many of them to remember details. He said, "So?"

"It wasn't my fight," Matt continued. "And I had a job to complete. I couldn't get involved in that fight. But as you laughed over the body, I swore that if our paths ever crossed, I'd avenge that young boy's senseless death. I think maybe that time is at hand."

"You talk big. What's your name?"

"Matthew Bodine. You can call me Mr. Bodine."

"You're a very funny man. Wonder if you'll be laughing when I kill you."

"I won't be as easy to kill as that boy."

"Maybe you have a little more experience. Maybe you even have the start of a reputation. None of that will help you when I plug you."

Matt knew that the other man was trying to play mind games with him. He could also play those games.

"I've seen you. I've heard about you. And I know I'm faster. Ask anybody."

Sam also sat easily on his horse. He looked around the crowd. Malinda had stepped to one side. The others knew enough to get out of the way of fire, but they acted as if they were stuck to their places on the street. Sam knew that Matt had bit off a big cud to chew this time, but he would not interfere in a fight between Matt and Caphorn, since a matter of honor was at stake. But he was prepared to keep the fight fair.

"Ask me," Sam said, "I think you're probably a tad too self-important. I'd bet money that Matt is faster than you."

"And who asked you?" Caphorn said.

"He did," Sam joked, pointing to Matt.

"You must be Sam Two-Wolves. You're both funny, funny, funny."

"Prove yourself," Matt said. "I'm ready anytime you are."

"You have your friends backing you up," Caphorn said.

"They won't draw. This is between you and me."

The hands of neither Matt nor Caphorn had moved a fraction of an inch. Both were still near their guns, ready to draw and shoot cold death in an instant. For an instant, Matt thought that his opponent would draw. Instead, Caphorn slowly moved his hand away from his gunbelt.

"I'll oblige you and kill you," Caphorn said. "But it'll be in my own good time. At my profit."

"Maybe I should just shoot you now," Matt replied, just as cool. "It'd save me the trouble of having to hunt you down after you try and shoot me in the back."

"No, boy. I'll face you. And I'll kill you." He touched his hand to his hat. "Until that time, I bid you good day."

Caphorn laughed, turned his back to the crowd, and walked away. Matt remained on his horse for long seconds. The air was still, as if the crowd was holding its collective breath, wondering which of the two shootists would die. If the tense episode bothered Matt, he didn't show it. He waited a few more seconds before stepping out of the saddle to the ground. In an almost identical movement, Sam also stepped off his horse.

In a low voice, Sam said, "I thought for a moment there he was going for his gun."

"Yeah."

"Think he chickened out?"

"I wouldn't underestimate him. We'll have to face each other. You can count on that."

Jordan stepped forward, and said in a friendly sounding voice, "I'm so glad you found Malinda!" He reached his hand out to the woman. "And you weren't hurt!" He pulled her to him. She responded stiffly. Jordan spotted her bruises, and continued, "They hurt you a little. That's too much." He acted as if he were thinking a moment, then added, "You can rest tonight. No show tonight. I'll get word out. Though you as much as asked for it, spending time with these Hart supporters . . ."

The woman pulled her hand away and

walked inside. The crowd was still quiet, but started to come awake. This time Hart stepped forward and raised his voice.

"This has gone too far," he said. "You've stepped over the line."

"I don't have any idea what you mean," Jordan said.

"You've tried every other means to get my claims. You even brought in some guns. But now you've brought in the likes of Caphorn."

"Hart, my man, you've gone over the edge . . ."

But Hart had stepped out of the crowd, fists swinging. Suddenly the fight was taking place on the street.

It was dark in Jordan's mine shaft. There was surprisingly little activity going on in the digs, though Parrish could hear a few of Jordan's men talking deep in the hole. They would probably die when the mine caved in, but that would be alright. It would stir things up even more.

Parrish didn't realize that Malinda had already been found and brought back to town. Even had he known, he would have been satisfied with his work. Even if some doubts existed, the idea had been set that one of Jordan's men had taken potshots at

Bodine. The rumor had also taken hold that it was Bodine or some other of Hart's men who had taken Malinda. The shooting would have to start soon. This destruction of Jordan's mine would surely be the final straw!

Parrish had never done any real work in his life, and certainly not with explosive or in a mine. He had seen it done, and heard miners talk about it, however. So he thought, *How hard could it be?* He fumbled in the darkness, trying to determine the best place to put the explosives. He wasn't even sure how much to use. He had stolen plenty — more than he could easily carry and sneak into town and into the mine. Parrish figured he had enough to do the job.

He placed some in various crevices, and then at the mine entrance.

And what about the fuses? He had tried to arrange it so that they could all feed off of one main line. And that would be a long one, since he wanted to be a safe distance away when the explosion occurred. What if one fizzled out? He decided to have two lines coming out of the mine entrance. He would set them both off. Surely at least one would work!

Parrish placed the fuse, started to feed it out as he went toward the fading daylight outside the entrance. He suddenly heard a movement. Parrish froze, his back to the cool wall of the mine.

The sounds were coming from the mine entrance. It was a faint sound of footsteps on gravel, though it sounded louder to Parrish. He waited, hoping that no other miner would enter. Or maybe the gunfighter was hidden well enough? He could shoot, though that would give him away.

The footsteps moved slowly, quietly, as if the person also didn't want to be seen or heard.

A shadow crossed the mine shaft opening. The man then stepped to the entrance, stuck his head in to look around.

It was Shannahan.

Parrish cursed to himself. He should have killed that crazy Irishman when he had the chance! Shannahan had been trying to dog Parrish's every move. He had so far managed to avoid Shannahan, but it was getting damned tiring! Why couldn't he just stick to his mining, like he was supposed to? Well, Parrish thought, he'd take care of the Irishman sooner or later.

Shannahan knew he was on dangerous ground — one of Hart's men on Jordan ground. That was why he was moving so quietly. Parrish thought this might even work in his favor. As far as he knew, nobody had seen him enter the mine. Maybe somebody would see Shannahan sneaking around, and think he had set the explosion. What could be better?

Shannahan was at the mine entrance for only a few moments. He acted as if he might investigate further, but stopped before he had set one foot in the mine. He tipped his head as if he heard something, uttered a few words that Parrish couldn't understand, then started to run back toward the center of town.

Parrish relaxed. Nobody else seemed to be around. He bent down and continued to feed out the fuse.

He paused at the mine entrance, looked all around to make sure he was alone, then stepped outside. Now that he was in the open, he worked quickly to finish the job.

Parrish ran the end of the fuse to behind a pile of rubble near the mine. His horse was tied and waiting for him to get away. From town came sounds of fighting. Maybe the war had already started, even without this latest addition? No matter, this would guarantee the results.

The men inside the mine would soon be leaving, if they hadn't started out already.

Now was the time.

Parrish struck a match, touched the flaming head to the fuses.

They started to sputter and spark.

Parrish mounted his horse and fled the scene so he would not be caught in the explosion.

Hart wasn't sure what had come over him. He hadn't planned to fight with Jordan that evening. When Sam and Matt had brought in Malinda, basically unharmed, it looked as if another potentially dangerous confrontation might be defused.

Still, feelings on both sides were running high. The bodies that the two blood brothers brought back didn't help matters any, since some of them had friends in town.

But then, when he saw the new gun that Jordan had brought in, Hart could stand it no longer. He knew that Phil Caphorn was in a league apart from the usual run-of-the-mill gunslingers. He was ruthless, and he was expensive. In itself it was probably no better or worse than other tricks that Jordan had played, but it was enough to push Hart over the edge. His raging temper, which he had kept in check, now boiled over.

He was not swinging wildly. He had some professional training, had sometimes sparred with Shannahan, but had also learned in some tough saloons. He had a lifetime of hard work in his muscles. His first punch was flawless. It moved through the air as quickly and silently as a bird through the air, but landed against Jordan's chin with a loud *whump.* Jordan took a step back and would have fallen to the ground if not for the hotel wall.

The punch seemed to unleash trapped energy on both sides, as the groups fell into a free-for-all.

Somebody grabbed Hart from behind. He didn't bother to even look who had made such a dumb move. Hart simply shrugged his massive shoulders, loosening the grip on his arms. He then elbowed the man behind him. The punch knocked the breath out of the other man. Hart followed up with an upward thrust of his elbow, knocking the other man to the ground.

Shannahan came running. He picked up one of Jordan's men and slammed him bodily to the ground. Shannahan stepped on him and used him as a jump-off point to pull down a third man.

Sam and Matt looked at each other, then both ducked some punches thrown their way. They grabbed the arms of their two attackers and threw them into the middle of the mob scene.

The horses pawed the ground nervously. Somebody loosened the ropes that held the dead men on the horses, and the bodies fell to the ground. One of Jordan's men didn't see the bodies in time, and tripped over them. He was kicked in the head as he went down, and didn't get back up.

"How come we always find ourselves in the middle of this kind of thing?" Matt asked Sam, as he dodged the punches of another attacker.

"I was wondering the same thing," Sam answered. "You'd think a couple of smart fellows like ourselves would learn sooner or later."

"Well, it was your idea to stay," Matt said, ducking and weaving.

"*My* idea! You were the one who got sweet on that singer . . ."

Matt found the opening he had been looking for, and snaked out with a left that felled his opponent.

"Yeah, but you agreed to it!"

"True. That was a good punch, though."

"Thank you."

Jordan, though he had received a solid punch, was young and in good physical condition. Though dazed at first, he quickly recovered and came back at Hart. He did not have the power that Hart had, but he was persistent. His blows seemed to come at Hart from all directions at once. At first one blow, then another, pounded the older man.

Like an old bull, Hart just kept coming. He clenched his fists together and swung. They connected with Jordan's chest. Their combined force again sent him reeling.

Strep had barely moved from the spot where he was standing before the fight had started. He was sore from his fight earlier with Matt. He was tired from his search for Malinda. He was still angry from Jordan's less-than-kind words for his part in bringing Malinda safely home. So he contented himself with protecting himself with an occasional well-placed jab and checking to make sure that Jordan was not in any potentially fatal danger. He still worked for Jordan, but he was wondering just how far his loyalty would stretch.

Caphorn had stopped down the street, outside of the area where the fighting was taking place, and watched the action with amusement. His only concern was that Jordan might get killed before Caphorn could receive his payment. On the other hand, if that were to happen, Caphorn wouldn't have to face Bodine. It was not that Caphorn was scared. He had been the top dog for so long that he couldn't even conceive of not winning. Still, there was something in Bodine's eyes that caused Caphorn to have a slight twinge of doubt, for the first time in many years. And he didn't like that feeling.

Jordan was now very angry. He grabbed Hart's arms and growled, "I've been nice up to now. Now you've really asked for it. And I'm going to give it to you."

In answer, Hart forced Jordan back to the ground.

Suddenly a shot rang out.

"Who the hell is stupid enough to start shooting in this kind of close quarters?" Sam asked.

"Who knows. Who cares."

Both men knew that in this kind of close quarters, a stray bullet was more dangerous than a well-aimed one. Each hit the ground to avoid any loose lead that might be flying around. Somebody else returned the fire, and the rest of the group also scurried for cover. Even Strep abandoned his place.

Shots started to blast from what seemed like all directions at once. Their whine could be clearly heard as they passed. But whoever was shooting apparently had bad aim, for none of the bullets hit anything but the hotel wall.

All the shooting was suddenly over-whelmed by a larger blast.

The explosion filled the evening air, drowning out the sharper sounds of gunfire.

When the roar of the explosion died down, the gunshots had also stopped. Somebody shouted, "The mine!"

Hart clenched his teeth and was ready to go after Jordan again. He said, "So you had to destroy my mine. Alright. Now I will have to kill you. If you've hurt any of my men, you'll die a slow death . . ."

Matt glanced up and down the street. He hollered, "Hey! The smoke's coming from Jordan's mine!"

Hart had Jordan's shirt collar in his fist as he prepared to pummel him with his other fist. At the sound of Matt's words, his fist released its grip and Jordan slumped back against the wall.

Almost as one, the crowd temporarily forgot its fight and moved toward Jordan's mine.

CHAPTER FIFTEEN

Matt and Sam were toward the front of the crowd, followed by Hart. Jordan and Strep were not far behind. Only minutes had passed from the time of the explosion to the arrival of the crowd at the mine site. Dust was still drifting from the sky, covering the rocks and pieces of timber that now littered the ground. A wide area around the mine entrance had collapsed, leaving a shallow depression.

Sam was watching Jordan out of the corner of his eye. He was surprised to see him so calm. At first, Jordan acted almost indifferent, as if he had joined the crowd out of idle curiosity. As he started to survey the wreckage, he became agitated and turned to Hart.

"Damn you, Hart! You accuse me of all kinds of crimes, and here you are, destroying my mine! This really means war, now . . ."

Hart had his back to Jordan. Sam was prepared to intervene if Jordan tried to shoot the other man in the back. Hart seemed to not realize the danger he had put himself in.

Hart said, "Just shut up, Jordan."

Jordan started to reach for a gun he wore under his coat. Sam stepped forward and put a solid hand on Jordan's arm. He didn't say a word. Strep looked to Jordan for instructions.

"I'll find you one of these days without your bodyguards," Jordan said. "When I do, I'll show you what happens when you push me too hard."

"Just stop shooting off that mouth for a second, will you?" Hart asked. "You can't possibly think I caused this explosion?"

Hart's tone of voice also surprised Sam. The miner was now talking as some of his Eastern college professors had done when discussing a problem. It was a mixture of matter-of-fact with a touch of discovery.

"Of course you set it, you bastard."

Hart continued, "If you were a professional mining engineer — or even a half-baked one, for that matter — instead of an empty-headed, big-city lawyer, you'd know I couldn't possibly have done this job. It's just too shoddy."

"You son-of-a-bitch . . ."

Sam tightened his hand around Jordan's arm in a vicelike grip. "I agree with Hart. Shut up for a minute. I want to hear this."

Strep took a step toward Sam, then seemed to change his mind. He stepped into the crowd and started questioning some of the men who had worked in the mine.

"I've been in and around mines since I was old enough to walk," Hart said. "I can set an explosion that would bring down a mountain or blow a fly from a cow turd and not get any shit on me. You understand? If I had wanted to destroy your mine, I would have destroyed it." He walked to the mine entrance, picked up a piece of the rubble. "Look at the damage. Some of the explosive went out from the mine, hurting little except the surrounding dirt. Oh, it caved in the entrance, and probably some of your tunnel. But no serious damage with lasting consequences."

Matt stepped forward. "All that's well and good, but a more important question is whether or not any men were in the mine at the time."

Sam watched Jordan's expression with interest. Jordan, still acting as if he were angry, paused and said more calmly, "Fortunately, as you might know, I've been moving my major operations to a different site. That means there were probably no men in the mine at the time of the explosion."

Strep yelled to Jordan, "There are at least two men unaccounted for, maybe three. They may still be in the mine!"

"I hardly think so . . ."

Sam wondered. His keen ears seemed to pick up some kind of sound, as if from a great distance. It could have been voices. He stepped forward, placed his head on the ground at the mine entrance.

It was definitely voices he had heard. Men yelling in terror at being pinned under the ground. A cold chill went up Sam's spine. He knew his own feelings about being underground. He could only imagine what it would be like to be trapped.

He bent over, picked up a huge rock. He strained, then with a mighty push hurled it out of the way. He followed with a second rock, then a third one.

Hart looked up from his studies. "Sam! What are you doing?"

"There's men trapped in there. We've got to get them out."

"Jordan's men?"

"They're men. Just because they work for Jordan doesn't mean they automatically deserve to die. Are you going to help me, or not?"

Hart looked at Shannahan and his other men. He sighed, then suddenly he was the take-charge, hard-minded miner again. He barked orders to his men. "Get your shovels. Get your other tools. Let's get at least an air shaft to the men. If they're still alive, as Sam thinks, they'll run out of air in hours . . . if they're lucky."

Jordan started to protest. "Nobody's going to believe it. You set this explosion not just to destroy me but to make you look like some kind of hero . . ."

Sam said to Matt, "You watch my back. If any of these jokers try anything, please shoot them."

"Hell, Sam, you gave me the fun job."

"At least you can't say I'm never nice to you."

"This'll make up for leaving the camp for me to clean up!" Matt laughed. This time his laugh covered genuine concern, because he knew of Sam's feelings, and how courageous he was by leading the rescue effort.

Strep came forward, leading some of Jordan's other men. Matt said, "Hold it. You come any closer, and I'll kill you."

Strep reached down and picked up a shovel. "Hell, we're going to help, too."

As Jordan's men and other miners from the town temporarily forgot their arguments with Hart and his men and started to dig as well, Jordan saw that public opinion had turned against him, at least in this instance. Jordan also then half-heartedly joined in the effort. Matt also helped in the work, though he kept a vigilant eye on Strep and Jordan.

The rock and soil worked its way into Sam's clothes. It caked his neck, back, and arms. It seemed to fill his nose and scratched his eyes. He tossed his hat to Matt, and tied a bandanna around his head to keep the sweat from his eyes.

The larger rocks that were loose he moved to one side using only the strength of his hands and arms. Others he had to pry out. Slowly a hole was again being sunk into the mine. But was it enough? Would he be able to make it in time?

He listened closer, but he had dug himself into a hole. He could now only hear his own heavy breathing, his heart beating, and the sounds of the others working around him.

Sam had not been sure he believed in the old Cheyenne gods since he had witnessed the slaughter of his own people as well as the slaughter at the Little Big Horn. He was not sure he even accepted the white man's God. But as he worked to save people he didn't even know, who might in other circumstances hate him and want to kill him, he gave a few unspoken requests for help. He had never been sure why he had done some of the things he had done, though he had always done what he believed to be right. No matter how crazy the actions seemed to outsiders.

This was one of those instances. The ground seemed to be closing in around him. He hated to be in such a tight spot, with no escape route.

He pushed the feelings to one side, and continued to dig. He dug in the direction from where he thought he had heard the voices.

At the top of the new hole, Sam heard Hart ask, "Jordan, is he going in the wrong direction? Doesn't he need to go more toward the center, where the dirt and rocks might be less packed?"

"Hell if I know," Jordan said. "I'm not an engineer."

"You said it right."

Jordan said, angrily, "I have a man that does that job for me. Strep, find my engineer, Smithson."

"He's already gone for the maps," Strep said, pausing in his own digging.

Sam turned his attention back to the

ground. Map or no map, he thought he knew the direction to dig. It was a matter of instinct. His instincts had helped him too many times to count in his young life. He figured it would probably help him out again.

Sam wasn't sure how he had done it, but he was pulling ahead of the other men. It was now getting even tighter. It was difficult to maneuver his shovel. In frustration and anger, he started to pound a spot where the dirt seemed to be more loosely packed.

A tiny spot crumpled into itself.

Sam pounded harder around the edges.

The tiny spot dissolved into a larger hole beneath his feet.

Sam pried more rocks loose, forcing the hole bigger. As he dug, he could hear the rocks falling through the hole and bouncing into the shadows below.

"I think I've got an opening!" Sam said. "Send me down a rope!"

"Don't do it, Sam," Hart said. "If you go down now, you could also be trapped. Let us dig out some more, to make sure it won't cave in on you."

"No. The men down below can't wait."

"Send him down a rope," Matt said. "He's made up his mind. If he doesn't get his way, he may come up shooting."

Somebody tossed the rope down to Sam.

Holding his breath, thinking about the wide open skies of his ranch, Sam lowered himself into the pit.

Malinda was in the hotel when she heard the explosion. She ran to the window. She watched as the crowd suddenly started rushing toward Jordan's mine site. A few minutes later, some of the men came wandering back, talking excitedly among themselves.

She called down and asked, "What's going on?"

She didn't recognize either of the two men. One said, "Somebody's blown up the mine!"

"Which one?"

"Jordan's."

She thought a second, then continued, "What's happening now?"

"It's the damndest thing," the second man said. "Excuse my language, ma'am. It's one of the craziest things I've ever seen. Some men are trapped in the mine. That half-breed Injun and his friend are leading the rescue effort. And that Hart is helping!"

The two men shook their heads, as if they couldn't understand such an unusual situation.

"Why aren't you men helping?"

"Why should we? We've got our own claims to work. Why should we help Jordan or Hart?"

The two continued walking, talking to each other.

Malinda stepped back from the window, a crazy thought entering her mind. She would go down to the site and help as well! It would be out of character for her, which would make it even better. She was tired of doing what Jordan wanted her to do. Matt had showed her that sometimes it's important to take chances, to reach out for something new.

She looked to her clothes and realized she had nothing appropriate for such rough work. The closest she could come was a dress she sometimes used for her rides in the country. It would have to do.

It was only a short walk to the mine, but it was long enough that many men in town stopped and stared as she walked. At the mine entrance, men were working with picks and shovels. Matt was helping, though he was also keeping a watchful eye on Jordan and his men.

"Malinda!" Jordan bellowed. "You get back to the hotel!"

"I came to help," she said.

"Didn't you hear what I said? Get back. Now."

In response, Malinda bent down and tried to pick up a stone. It was heavier than it looked, and she almost dropped it. Matt walked over, took it from her hands.

Jordan hollered, "Malinda!"

Matt backhanded him, shutting him up quickly and effectively. He said to the woman, "I'm glad you came out to help. There's plenty of men here to dig. But they could sure use some water."

"I'll get some right now," Malinda said. She ignored Jordan as she walked away.

Jordan looked at Matt with hate in his eyes. Matt ignored Jordan, as well.

Hart joined Matt. "Guess I'm really ashamed of myself now," Hart said.

"Why?"

"Even that girl is helping out. And here I am doing hardly anything."

"You're digging."

"Yeah. I know. But Sam's down there by himself, and I know how he feels about being underground. If I went down there, I might be able to help with some of my engineering experience. Or with my strength. I don't like to brag, but I can hold my own with any man in this town, pound for pound."

"So what're you waiting for?"

"Wish us luck."

Sam had been concerned about being able to see down in the shaft, but his eyes adjusted to the gloom and enough light was now entering the opening that he could make out most of the features of the mine. As Hart had suggested, only the upper part of the mine had been blown. It had blocked the entrance, but further below, where Sam now was, little damage had occurred except for the rubble that had rolled onto the mine floor. He wondered if Hart could have set the explosion to allow himself to be a hero? If he did, then Sam was a bad judge of character, and Sam was seldom wrong about men.

Sam heard a faint moan just ahead of him in the shadows.

After a few more steps, Sam saw the men. One was spread-eagle on the floor. Blood was seeping from a wound on his head where a falling rock had hit it. Another was trapped beneath a support timber that had fallen.

Sam examined the bleeding man. He was breathing, but barely. Sam ran back the short distance to the opening.

"Send down a pry bar!" He shouted.

"While you're doing that, I'm sending one of the men up. He's still alive, but unconscious!"

He hurried back to the unconscious man. Behind him, he heard the metallic clatter of the pry bar as it was tossed down to him. Sam picked up the big underground miner as if he were a child. At the opening, he secured the rope around him as best he could. Sam knew that the move might kill the injured man, but it was the only chance he had to live.

As the men above worked the unconscious man back to the surface, Sam picked up his pry bar and returned to the trapped miner.

"Can you hear me?" Sam asked. "Can you understand?"

The other man groaned, but shook his head. He opened his eyes. His face was caked with grime.

Sam looked over the timber. It was about ten feet long, and had somehow wedged itself tight against the mine wall. Sam pushed, but it wouldn't budge an inch. He worked his pry bar underneath it at the end away from the miner. This time it moved a fraction of an inch, but increased the pressure on the trapped man. He groaned louder.

Sam removed the pry bar to reconsider.

Behind him he heard the sound of falling rocks. He looked back just as Hart appeared from the swirling dust. He was also holding a heavy bar that he could use for leverage in moving the timber.

"What are *you* doing down here?" Sam asked.

"Part of the truth is that you made me damned ashamed up there," Hart said. "This feud with Jordan has me so rattled I forgot that there's more to this life than gold and silver ore. A man's life is worth something. Even the men of the enemy. I thought maybe my experience and knowledge could make this job a little easier for you."

"I didn't think you had that in you. I didn't know anybody in this town did."

"Of course, the rest of the truth is that this would be the first — and maybe only chance — I'd have to take a firsthand look at Jordan's diggings. I don't think there's much ore here, but you never know."

Sam laughed. "Well, at least you're honest. And I could use your help."

Hart looked over the situation, and quickly realized the problem.

"I'll take this end, protect this man's leg, while you pry from that end. With luck, we'll be able to loosen the timber enough for him to get out."

Sam knew that Hart was a strong man, but he didn't realize how strong until he applied his full force to the log. He almost single-handedly made it crunch and protest, but finally it gave way an inch . . . two inches . . . three inches. Sam applied his own force and the log suddenly raised another inch.

Except the groaning had stopped. The man had fainted and could not move under his own power.

Hart also saw the situation. Sam watched with unbelieving eyes as Hart slowly moved position. He shifted so that only one arm was now holding the log. The muscles in his arm were like steel bands. With his free hand, he slowly reached down and yanked the unconscious man free of the timber. The move awakened the man to pain, but at least he was alive and free.

Almost as if they had been working together for years, Hart and Sam released their hold on the timber simultaneously. It crashed to the mine floor, sending up another shower of dust.

CHAPTER SIXTEEN

Dust filled the small space, covering Sam, Hart, and the miner they had just saved. The heavy timber falling to the floor of the mine sounded almost like an explosion. It made Sam feel as if the walls were closing in on him, sending a chill up his back. The last thing Sam wanted was to be buried underground. He forced himself to remain calm. Hart acted unconcerned.

"Is there any danger of another cave-in?" Sam asked.

"Oh, there's always a danger, but I think in this case the danger is slight," Hart answered. "Even with the explosion, this still seems pretty solid. It'd still be a good idea to get out of here as quickly as we can."

"I'll go along with that."

"How's our man doing?"

The dust had now settled enough that Sam could again see clearly. He kneeled beside the miner, who was trying to keep the pain from showing in his face. He wasn't doing a very good job. His face was pale and covered with grime. He let his breath out sharply when Sam checked out his leg.

"It's broken," Sam said to the miner. "But I've seen a lot worse. What about your other leg? Can it stand any weight at all?"

"I'll try it and see," the miner said.

He put his good leg under him, and stood slowly. Sam and Hart let the miner support his weight on them.

"Any more down here besides you and the other fellow we've already gotten out?"

"No . . . there was just Clyde and me."

They walked to the opening, which was getting larger by the minute. As they came into the slightly brighter light, the miner took a closer look at Sam and Hart. He said in surprise, "You're that half-breed, Two-Wolves. And you're . . . Clarence Hart." He shook his head, as if to clear it. "I think I must be delirious."

Sam said, "You're doing just fine."

"This is crazy. I was in that crowd that fought you a little while back. If I had the chance, I probably would've killed you. So why'd you save my life?"

"Beats me why I do some of the things I do. Maybe I was born crazy."

The miner's face was still pale beneath

the dirt, but he was acting stronger without the weight of the timber resting on his leg.

"I sure had it wrong about you, and I'll admit," he said. "I can tell you one thing. If shooting between you guys starts again, I'm going to be sitting it out. Just because I work for Jordan doesn't mean I'll fight anybody on his say-so. Especially when they saved my life."

"I'm glad to hear that," Sam said. "I hate to see people sucked in on the wrong side, and have to pay for their mistake with their lives."

"A lot of other miners will agree with me. Once they see how you jumped in to help, they'll probably not lift a finger against you, either."

Hart called up. "Throw down another rope!" In seconds, another length of rope was lowered. Sam started to tie it around the miner, who was still leaning on Hart.

"A lot of us aren't too pleased with Jordan, anyway," the miner continued.

Hart asked, "He mistreat you boys?"

"Not any worse than a lot of other places. It's just that he doesn't seem very smart when it comes to mining. That's what me and Clyde was doing down here tonight. We couldn't believe our ears when we got the orders."

Sam tightened a knot in the rope. He asked, "What orders?"

"Jordan told us to move our operations. To abandon this mine because it didn't test out. But, hell, there's some good diggings down here. Nobody's found the main vein yet, but there's enough down here to make some tidy profits."

"There, that should do it," Sam said. "It'll probably hurt like the dickens while they're pulling you out."

"I can handle it. Go to it."

"Take him up!" Sam called out. The rope tightened, and the miner moved slowly up.

"You're next," Sam said.

"Not just yet. I want to look at something."

Sam shrugged, but followed Hart. The miner ran his hand along the rock wall, sometimes bringing his face close to it as if he were attempting to smell out the secrets of the rock. He finally found a spot that interested him. He had no hammer or chisel, so found a chunk of rock on the mine floor and struck it sharply against the rock wall. A small piece of stone fell off. Hart caught it and put it in his pocket.

He continued this sequence throughout the small, enclosed area. Finally, satisfied, he said, "I'm ready to go now."

"What's this all about?"

"These are samples I couldn't have gotten any other way. They might help me figure out where the main vein is and if I'm on the right track. I couldn't very well let such a golden opportunity slip by me."

"You're something else, Hart."

The miner tossed to the floor the stone he had been using as a chisel. It landed with a soft clink.

"I'd say it's time we got out of here. I feel like it's been a good day's work and it's time for a beer."

Strep paused in his work as Malinda approached him with a bucket of water. He had been surprised when the woman showed up to help in the rescue effort. He was even more surprised to see she was still around. During all the months that he had served as her informal bodyguard and driver, Strep had never seen the woman even hint at this side of her. She was a local celebrity, and she had acted as if she was a star. Strep knew Malinda was Jordan's girl, but he still had hoped against hope that she might someday acknowledge him as more than just one of Jordan's hired hands. Strep's gun was for hire, and he had not been particular in whom he had worked for.

Even so, there were points where he drew the line, and if he could get Malinda interested in him, his working for Jordan would be history.

No matter, during those months Malinda had done little but look down her nose on him.

Now, after only one outing with Matt Bodine, who seemed to Strep to be no better than a drifter, Malinda was acting as if she had a heart and a mind of her own.

No figuring women, Strep thought.

Malinda stopped in front of him and held out the bucket. Strep took the dipper from the bucket and took a drink.

"I want to thank you," Malinda said softly.

Strep almost choked on the water. "Thank me for what?" he asked.

"For helping find me," she said. "I'll admit I haven't thought much of you these past few months. You were just kind of invisible to me. And I'm not going to tell you any lies. You're not my type. But I appreciate your effort."

Strep gave back the dipper. He wanted to say something, but no words came out of his open mouth.

Malinda smiled and moved on to offer water to the next worker.

Strep stared after Malinda. His attention

was broken by Jordan's voice.

"That's disgusting," he said, lighting a fresh cigar. "Try to be nice to a woman, and they get out of control. Look at her, acting so *nice.* I'll take care of her later. In the meantime, Strep, I want you back at the hotel in about an hour."

Strep turned to Jordan. Still stunned by Malinda's words to him, he wasn't paying close attention to what Jordan was saying.

"What?"

"Don't tell me you got a case of the stupids, too," Jordan growled. "Do I have only imbeciles working for me? Be at the hotel in an hour. We've got some planning to do."

"What about the men trapped in the mine?"

Jordan spit a bit of tobacco to the street. "Have you gone soft in the head? One's out. The other'll be out soon enough. As if it made a difference."

Strep had about enough. He had served Jordan loyally. He had protected Jordan's woman, and helped to bring her safely back when she was kidnapped. He was still suffering from the bruises and cuts that he had suffered in his fight with Matt, trying to protect Jordan's investment. Strep's gun was for hire, but Jordan had taken it too far.

Jordan turned his back and was walking

back to the hotel.

Strep took a deep breath and considered his options. The only way he could be near Malinda was to work for Jordan. He hated Bodine, and the only other option in town was to side with him and Hart's men against Jordan. His only real choice was to stay with Jordan.

Back at the mine entrance, the second of the two trapped miners was pulled out of the hole to the ground.

Phil Caphorn had taken his place at the table he had selected, where he had drunk down most of the bottle in front of him. He liked his liquor, could hold it well, and it never seemed to bother his gunmanship.

Now he was thinking. Bodine's threats hadn't scared him. He had been threatened before by all kinds of men. They were now all six feet under. Still, there was something about Bodine that made Caphorn pause. He had faced tough men before. He had faced men who were speedy with a gun. So what was different about Bodine?

And then there was this crazy town. Caphorn had been listening to the gossip in the hotel saloon and how Bodine's partner, Sam Two-Wolves, had jumped into action to heroically save two men *trapped in Jordan's mine.* Who would be crazy enough to help his enemy?

More importantly, it seemed as if Jordan and Hart would have to confront each other. But Jordan was losing support. It would not make Jordan's efforts impossible, but perhaps more difficult.

Of course, in the end, that was irrelevant to Caphorn. He had been hired to do one thing, and one thing only. That was to kill Matt Bodine and Sam Two-Wolves. As soon as the gold was deposited in his bank account, Caphorn would meet the two blood brothers and kill them.

In the meantime, he had some time to kill.

He motioned to the bartender to bring him another bottle.

Sam had never valued the open skies as much as when he climbed out of the collapsed mine entrance. He hadn't realized how much being in the tight confinement had bothered him until he again breathed the fresh air and felt freedom.

By the time Sam had loosened the rope that had helped bring him out of the mine, the two miners who had been trapped were stretched out on the ground and being treated. A few of the workers patted Sam on the back. Much of the hostility that had existed before the explosion that caused the mine cave-in seemed to be forgotten.

Jordan would not forget. And Sam had no illusions that saving his men would cause a change in heart in Jordan. Sam looked around for the mine owner, but neither he nor his men were anywhere in sight.

Matt was talking with Malinda, who was carrying a water bucket. Sam knew that Matt would allow nothing, not even a pretty woman, to interfere with his executing his tasks flawlessly. But Sam couldn't resist needing Matt a little.

Sam stepped over to his blood brother. He said, "Hey, I thought you were supposed to be watching my back. And here you are with all your attention on a woman!"

"Well, hell, she's a sight prettier than your back!"

"But what if somebody wanted to bury me in the bowels of the earth?"

"Mother Earth would just kick you back out — you'd be indigestible!" Matt said.

Malinda shook her head and said, "You two are something else."

"Thanks for your help, Malinda," Matt said.

"Any time," Malinda answered politely as she walked away.

"Are you really falling for a saloon singer?"

Sam asked.

"She's not just a saloon singer," Matt answered. "But in answer to your question, I like her, sure. But it'll be a long time, if ever, before I ever consider settling down."

"Just wondering," Sam said.

With the excitement over, the crowd started to leave. Sam said, more seriously, "I don't think Hart set this explosion."

"I think you're right."

"And I don't see what benefit blowing up his own mine would provide to Jordan."

"Right again."

"So who's your guess about who set the explosives?"

"Our friend with the bullwhip who kidnapped Malinda."

"We need to find him."

"Even if we find him, I doubt that it will keep Jordan and Hart from trying to kill each other. It's gone too far to change now."

"I just want to find Parrish, and take care of him, once and for all."

CHAPTER SEVENTEEN

Parrish was disappointed. And he was angry. So far, none of his plans had worked. He wondered if Bodine and Two-Wolves were really that smart, or just damned lucky.

Parrish was watching the action at Jordan's mine from a position on top of a rocky hill at the edge of town. From this vantage point, he couldn't make out details or hear the talk. He could only see *Hart and Jordan working together* to free the men in the mine. Sam Two-Wolves was apparently taking the lead in the rescue effort. Instead of starting the two sides shooting at each other, so that Parrish could pick up the pieces, both sides were apparently working together.

What else could go wrong?

"Freeze, Parrish."

The gunfighter recognized the voice behind him.

"So you finally found me, Shannahan. You going to shoot me in the back?"

"Any reason why I shouldn't?"

"It's just not very sporting."

"And what you did to me in the river with your bullwhip was sporting?"

Parrish didn't answer the question. Instead, he said, "What are you going to do with me?"

"Stand up. Very slowly. And turn around to face me."

Parrish did as he was told. Shannahan was standing with a large-caliber, older handgun aimed at Parrish. Shannahan was holding the reins to Parrish's horse.

"We're going into town."

"For what purpose?"

"You and I are going to have a little fight."

Matt and Sam were still talking when they saw Parrish walking back into town. Behind him was Shannahan, holding a gun on him in one hand and the reins of Parrish's horse in the other hand.

"How do you like that?" Sam said. "Ask, and you shall receive."

"Shannahan got Parrish, and I didn't even hear any shots being fired."

"Look at the vermin I found in the rocks," Shannahan said. "He was so stupid, he didn't even hear me coming. Just as well. I didn't want to shoot him, anyway."

"What do you have in mind?" Sam asked. "We know he was the one behind the shots being fired at Matt, the kidnapping of Malinda, and probably the blowing up of Jordan's mine. I'm sure any one of a number of people would be glad to take this fellow off your hands"

"I'm sure they would, too," Shannahan said. "But I have another idea in mind. But I'll need your help, Sam."

"Name it."

"I'm still stinging from the whipping he gave me in the river. I want to face him in a fair fight. I want you to referee, make sure he doesn't pull anything underhanded."

Matt laughed. "I'd be surprised if he can do anything that's not underhanded," he said.

Shannahan asked, "Would you do that for me? It's a matter of honor."

Sam did not laugh. "I understand honor. I'd be the last to deny you the pleasure. When do you propose this match to take place?"

"Here. Now. In front of everybody in town."

"I'd be happy." He turned to Parrish. "You heard the man. Take off your gunbelt and put it over there by your horse. If you live through this fight, I'll let you ride away.

Though I wouldn't be surprised if some of Malinda's admirers didn't come looking for you, anyway."

Parrish looked confused. Shannahan was removing his shirt to reveal well-developed muscles. He wasn't big, but he was strong. Parrish removed his gunbelt, placed it gently near the horse. He stepped over to his horse, pretended to rub it as he quietly loosened his saddlebag without anybody noticing. He figured he might need an ace in the hole.

"So what are the rules?" he said, as he turned.

"Take your best shot," Shannahan said. "I'll still beat you."

A circle had started to form around the two men in the street. As word got around, several bets started to change hands. Even Jordan and Caphorn came out to see what the ruckus was all about.

Shannahan put up his fists and stood in a boxer's stance.

"Come on," he said. "I'm ready for you."

Parrish decided to leave his shirt on. He approached Shannahan warily, trying to get a feel for his movements and any potential weaknesses. The two men circled each other slowly.

Suddenly Shannahan's right fist moved in

a blur with two quick jabs. Both hit Parrish in the head. He bounced back, shocked. He hadn't seen the blows coming, he only felt them when they hit.

He started to watch a little closer now and missed the next blow. It was a left to the stomach. As Parrish moved, he struck out with his right, followed by his left. His right hit only air, but his left struck a glancing blow to Shannahan's ear. Shannahan danced back as if he hadn't felt a thing.

This wasn't Parrish's kind of fight. It was too fancy for his taste. He preferred old-fashioned street fighting. After all, Shannahan told Parrish to try anything he wanted.

Parrish moved in, dodging blows. He struck Shannahan's chest and stomach repeatedly, but they apparently had no effect on the Irishman. For each blow delivered by Parrish, Shannahan delivered a similar blow, with more effective results. Parrish started to feel the punches. He moved back, out of range.

Shannahan remained dancing around.

Parrish moved in again, this time trying to throw his punches at the other man's weaving head. Each punch was effectively blocked by the other man. Parrish couldn't see how Shannahan did it. He was quickly tiring from the effort of trying to break

Shannahan's defenses, much less from the repeated blows that kept landing on his body. As he tired, it seemed more of Shannahan's punches landed, draining him even more.

During this whole time, Sam remained neutral. He watched the two men fighting, but said nothing and did nothing to interfere. Parrish wondered what he would do if he tried something "underhanded." Maybe it was time to give it a try?

Shannahan reached out with a blow to the head. Parrish went with the punch, fell to the ground near his horse.

"Get on up," Shannahan said. "I'm not nearly through with you yet. This is just the start. You won't get off that easy."

Parrish moved slowly up as if he could barely move, using his horse for support. Shannahan, impatient, danced in closer. Parrish reached up to his saddlebags, as if for support, but slipped his hand inside the flap.

Matt was watching the fight with interest. So far, Shannahan was giving a good show. Matt was no boxer, but had seen enough to know when a good fighter was toying with another man. Had he wanted to, Shannahan could have knocked down Parrish at any time.

"Want to place a bet?" Hart said. "There's still a few who are betting on Parrish. The smart money is on Shannahan."

"No bets," Matt said. "Seems to me like there's no contest." He glanced down and was surprised to see a bullwhip, similar to Parrish's, in Hart's hand.

"What's this?" Matt asked.

"As you know, Shannahan's been looking for Parrish for quite awhile. He's been planning this for just as long. He thinks that Parrish is going to try to get smart. He wanted to be prepared, just in case."

"Does Shannahan know how to use that thing?"

"He's been practicing. He may not be as good as Parrish, but he can hold his own."

"Then why did he want Sam to referee?"

"You never know what a man like Parrish will pull. His weapons are primarily a gun and a whip. A whip Shannahan can handle. But a gunman he's not. It's always possible that Parrish would have a gun hidden somewhere. You never know."

"That is true."

"But I also think in some way Shannahan wanted Sam to know that he is not a coward and not a weakling. Though he appreciated Sam stepping in and helping on the day you guys arrived, Shannahan thought that he was somehow less of a man because another had to help him out of the tight spot."

"That's crazy," Matt said. "It took a helluva man to face Parrish, unarmed and by himself."

"You know that. I know that. But to Shannahan, it's a matter of personal honor. By having Sam 'referee,' Shannahan figured it would somehow make his victory that much better."

"A matter of honor," Matt said. "Hope it doesn't get him killed."

"Come on, Parrish," Shannahan said. He was barely breathing hard. "What are you waiting for?"

Parrish turned suddenly, the bullwhip in his hand. It snapped out, barely missing Shannahan's ear. The crack was loud in the air.

Sam stepped forward.

"That's out," he said. "If you don't put it down, I'll be forced to take it from your — probably dead — hands."

"No, that's alright," Shannahan said.

"No. I intend to keep this fight fair."

"Like I said. It's alright." Sam turned to see Hart handing a similar bullwhip to Shannahan. "If this piece of crap wants to raise the ante, that's his choice. I thought he might try something like this. So I made sure I was prepared."

Sam smiled and said, "Go to it, gentlemen."

Parrish stopped in mid-stride. What was going on here? He had given any number of whippings in his time, but had never faced another man armed in the same way. Well, how difficult could it be? He was the expert, after all. He would just show this stubborn Irishman how a real whipping felt.

The gunfighter loosened his wrist, popping the tip gently a few times to make sure it was working right. Shannahan was no longer dancing around, but moving around warily, holding his whip lightly in his hand.

Parrish struck out, but his whip did not pop this time. Instead, Shannahan's whip also struck out, blocking the first whip's movement. The tips of both whips landed on the ground. But before Parrish could move, Shannahan had his leather in the air. It lashed through the air, landing on Parrish's right shoulder. The gunfighter heard the whistling of the whip, felt the sharp pain. He looked down, saw his shirt was torn and that blood had been drawn.

A blood-red anger seethed through Parrish, and he started cracking his whip like the devil himself. It sounded like a series of gunshots as he struck out at Shannahan. Parrish was pleased to see blood on the Irishman's cheek, though he had yet to land a solid blow. It seemed that his coordination was off, that his power was far less than it usually was, that his reaction time was extremely slow.

Then he realized the trap that Shannahan had set for him. His repeated blows to Parrish's body and head had exhausted him, reduced his strength and his reflexes. It kept Parrish from working at his usual level of ability, while Shannahan was still relatively fresh.

Parrish snapped his whip several more times, but his muscles felt like they were turning to rubber. In the fights he had been in, he had never taken such a beating and remained standing. He had never had to fight for such a long period of time without a rest.

As if sensing Parrish's weakness, Shannahan moved in. His whip started popping. It landed repeatedly on Parrish, tearing his shirt to pieces, making bloody the material that was left. The pain started to build in Parrish's body, joining with his fatigued muscles to scream in agony.

Almost in a panic, Parrish lashed out with

a blow that entwined the tip of his whip with that of Shannahan's. For a moment, they were knotted together, making each of them useless. Parrish jerked his hand, pulling the whip from Shannahan's hand. Parrish tossed down the useless whips, and dived at the Irishman. He grabbed Shannahan's knees, forcing him to the ground. He moved in, tried to land blows on the man beneath him. Shannahan still somehow managed to block them, even from his difficult position on the ground.

Shannahan arched his back, then flipped the other man over his head. In seconds, the Irishman was back on his feet. He reached down, grabbed the bullwhips, shook his loose.

"How's it feel to be on the receiving end?" Shannahan asked. His whip popped repeatedly, though his blows landed lightly. He could have killed Parrish any time he wanted to, but his purpose was more to teach him a lesson than to kill him.

Parrish tried to get away from the blows, which seemed to hurt far worse than they should have for landing no harder than they were. He crawled, tried to run, then fell under the barrage that never seemed to stop.

Finally, he was where he wanted to be. His holster was only a few feet away, with the handle facing him within easy reach.

He rolled the remaining few feet, managed to touch the gun handle when he heard Sam's voice, "Stop right there, Parrish. Make another move, and I'll shoot you."

Parrish glanced up to see Shannahan standing quietly, whip in his hand. Not far from him was Sam. His gun hand was steady, inches from his gun, ready to draw and shoot if Parrish made any further move for his gun.

CHAPTER EIGHTEEN

Sam had tried to keep the fight fair, and had, up to a point. Though Parrish was not a boxer, he managed to hold his own well enough. When Parrish pulled out his whip, Sam started to step in and stop the fight, until he saw Shannahan pull out a whip of his own. It was then that he decided to pull back and let nature take its course.

Now it was time to step in again.

Parrish's gun was still in its holster, on the ground where he had placed it before the fight started. His hand was on the handle of the gun, ready to pull it out and use it on Shannahan. This time, the Irishman was not equally armed and Sam was not about to let him be killed in cold blood.

"Hold it right there, Parrish," Sam said. His voice was cold and cut through the air like the whips had earlier.

Parrish paused, his fingers barely touching the gun handle. It might as well have been inches or feet for all the good it would do him now. Sam was fast, maybe as fast as Parrish in a fair fight. But Sam now had the drop on the gunfighter.

Shannahan looked over at Sam, as well. The Irishman had a puffy eye and a bloody mouth from the fight. The gunfighter, however, looked worse. His entire face was puffed out and bloody. His clothes were torn, with streaks of blood showing where the whip had touched him. His hair was matted with sweat and blood.

"This is my fight, Sam," Shannahan said. "I've been looking for this yahoo for days. You stay out of this."

"No can do, my friend," Sam answered. "I respect your need to fight for your honor. I feel you've given this fellow back all he gave you — and more. But I'm not going to let him shoot you."

Shannahan blinked, his fighting blood still raging through his veins. He took a deep breath, and seemed to see clearly again. He saw Parrish's hand on the gun.

"He can try it," Shannahan said grimly. "But I'm through fighting nice. This time I'll kill him with my bare hands."

He held up his strong hands, calloused from work and many fights. Sam had no doubt that those hands could break a man's neck. Sam knew that Parrish was quick and clever. He could still draw fast enough to plug the Irishman before he could get his hands around the gunfighter's neck.

"Flesh and blood are no match against lead," Sam said. "You've done your part. You've taught Parrish a lesson. Now it's time he was taught his final lesson. Maybe it'll demonstrate clearly the futility of trying to go against me or my brother."

"Speak English."

"I'm going to kick butt, and show anybody watching what'll happen if they cross us."

Sam had directed this last comment to Phil Caphorn, who had been watching the fight in silence. He knew better than to think it would worry Caphorn, but it might make him pause. It might be the slight advantage he or Matt would need.

Sam continued, "I have some beefs to pick with Parrish, as well. Matters like blowing up a mine. Like kidnapping Malinda, which caused a shooting fight that could have caused me to get killed. Like shooting at my brother. That gives me enough claim to Parrish."

Shannahan's breathing had become easier as he calmed down. Parrish's hand remained on the tip of the gun handle.

"Alright, Sam, you can shoot this dog if

you want."

Shannahan stepped back into the crowd, where Hart was waiting with a towel and a bucket of water. The Irishman started to dry himself off. The crowd seemed to move farther back, out of the line of fire, leaving Parrish more alone than ever on the ground in the middle of the street.

Caphorn was leaning against a post on the porch of the Jordan Hotel, watching the fight with interest. In his pocket was a message from his banker that arrived a little earlier, telling him the gold had arrived safely. He could now confront Sam and Matt when he felt like it. He was waiting now to hear Jordan's plans and to watch how Sam and Matt handled the fight between Shannahan and Parrish. Caphorn figured that Parrish would make short work of the Irishman. After all, Parrish had a small reputation, and who had ever heard of Shannahan?

Parrish had been a disappointment. Just another man who was a little faster with a gun than most others, but who lacked what it took to be a real fighter.

Caphorn was amused at Sam's talk, which Caphorn knew had been directed at him. He had seen various men partner at different times in the West, but the bond that existed between Sam Two-Wolves and Matt Bodine was unusual. They worked together well. They trusted each other. More importantly, they seemed to like each other.

And there was some other element that Caphorn could not define. It was something beyond his experience and understanding. Even now, Caphorn watched as Matt moved quietly, without comment or drawing attention to himself, to back up Sam. Matt was positioning himself to get a clear shot at Parrish should he try something else sneaky. Caphorn knew instinctively, however, that he would not double-team Parrish, as many other men would. Sam had called the fight, so Matt would not interfere, though he would not hesitate to attack if Parrish broke the unspoken rules even a little.

What was even more impressive to Caphorn was that Matt had also positioned himself to keep an eye on him, as well.

Matt was very clever. He was the one who had initially challenged Caphorn. He was the one Caphorn would have to face first. Though he had been paid to kill Matt and Sam, Caphorn knew that he would not have to go looking for Sam. Where ever Matt was, Sam would also be backing him up.

These two men made quite a team, with a bond that seemed stronger than blood.

In a way, it would be a kind of a shame to kill such unusual men. But, then, a job was a job, and this would help his reputation. It would help keep the gold flowing into his bank account, which was the most important thing.

Now, Matt had positioned himself and was apparently ignoring Caphorn. The gunfighter knew, however, that if he made a move for his gun, he would be facing flying lead from Matt, and then probably also from Sam.

Caphorn kept his hands in his plain sight. He wasn't ready yet to deal in death with Matt and Sam.

That time would come soon.

Very soon.

Parrish listened to Sam's talk, his hand motionless on the gun handle. He wished now that he had taken Jordan's original advice and left town. Maybe his reputation would be tarnished, but at least he would be alive.

He couldn't believe all his plans had failed, that it had come to this.

Ridiculed by Jordan, fired by him as if he were an ordinary employee and not a hired gun.

Beaten twice, once by Sam and once by Shannahan.

Now he was trapped like a rat, with no escape.

The gunfighter knew he was fast. It had made his reputation. But Sam was also fast. Sam and his partner, Matt, also had *something* that set them apart from all the other men he had faced. They laughed and enjoyed life and faced death as if they had no fear of death. They faced fistfights, mine cave-ins and shoot-outs with the same easy style that they brought to their drinking and partying.

Parrish felt a sinking feeling in his stomach. He was in a corner. He would have to shoot it out with Sam. He had been called. If he slithered away now, he would truly be a laughingstock. Nobody would take him seriously.

He could just as well be dead.

"Well, Parrish?" Sam said. "This has gone on long enough. You have the reputation as a gunfighter. Let's see you put your money down."

"You have the edge on me," Parrish said, trying to keep his voice steady. He was very tired, hurting from his beatings, and he was getting more and more worried. He thought maybe he could talk his way out of this situation.

"I know it," Sam answered. "I'm not one to take an unfair advantage. I'll give you a fair chance."

"That's sporting of you."

"I think so, too," Sam said. "You're as bad as Jordan, maybe worse. I should just shoot you and not worry about it. But I'm giving you a chance. That's more than I should probably do."

"What's your proposition?"

"Pick up your gunbelt. Strap it on. If you're as fast as you think you are, you shouldn't have any worry."

"What about Bodine?"

"He'll stay out of it, unless you try something underhanded. Then he'll shoot you and be happy about it. He took it kind of personal when you took his girl."

"She's not my girl!" Matt protested.

"Whatever," Sam said.

"Do I have a choice?" Parrish asked.

"You always have a choice. If you want to get on your horse and ride, I won't stop you. But then everybody in the West will know you're a coward. And I wouldn't be surprised if our paths still cross at some point. I have a long memory."

Parrish breathed deeply, trying to calm his

jangled nerves.

"Alright," he said. "I'll move slowly."

Parrish moved his hand back from the gun, got his feet under him and stood slowly. He felt like every eye in town was on him. If he had any thoughts of running, they had now fled. He flexed his fingers. They were a little stiff and sore, but they still worked. His arm was tired, but he felt like his years of practice and experience would still save him. He tried to calm his mind.

Sam stood quietly, in a relaxed posture, his arms crossed in front of him.

Parrish kneeled, picked up the gunbelt. He had worn the belt and the gun for years. It felt familiar to him, almost comforting. Sam had gotten a few lucky breaks. How did he think he could beat Parrish at his own game?

He strapped the belt around him. The weight of the holster against his thigh gave him even more confidence. He situated it just right, bent slowly with open palms to tie it down.

"Let me check the gun, will you?" he said.

Sam nodded.

Parrish noted that Matt was apparently watching him even closer than was Sam.

He thought, *Damn those two!* And damned the day he had ever crossed their paths.

Parrish moved his hand slowly, smoothly pulled his gun from his holster with fingers and thumb. The weight of the gun sent a new wave of optimism through him. He removed the shells, blew out any dust that might be in the chambers, inserted new bullets. He carefully checked the action, cocking the gun.

All the while he was also watching Sam, who stood motionless, arms still crossed in front of him.

This might be Parrish's only chance. Nobody could uncross his arms, draw his gun, and shoot faster than a man with a cocked gun already in his hand.

In a smooth, fluid motion, almost faster than the eye could see, Parrish shifted position. The gun in his hand almost aimed itself at the man standing down the street from him.

Parrish was pulling the trigger when he felt the first slug hit him in the chest.

He couldn't believe his eyes. Sam had also shifted his position as his hand dropped to his own gun. He pulled it and fired the first shot in a blur of motion that didn't register with Parrish until the lead hit him.

He pulled the trigger, but the bullet hitting him ruined his aim. The shot went wide and high.

He shot twice more. Those shots also went wild.

Sam's shots were more accurate. He placed three more bullets in a tight pattern in Parrish's chest. The gunfighter looked down in disbelief as blood started to squirt from his chest onto the street.

He tried to shoot again, but the gun was heavy in his hand and fell into the dirt.

As Parrish collapsed, he saw that Matt had also pulled his gun, but had not shot.

Parrish's last thought before he died was, *Nobody could be that fast.*

Sam stood quietly as Parrish fell to the street.

Matt also watched, until he was certain Parrish would not make another move. He holstered his gun and walked over to Sam.

"One down," he said. "How many more to go?"

"At least two," Sam answered. "I don't think Caphorn will back off. My guess is he's getting paid big bucks by Jordan. This demonstration might stop some, but from what I hear about Caphorn, I doubt if it'll stop him."

"And I don't think Jordan will back off, either," Matt said. "I have an idea he's going to pull something, but heck if I know what. With some of the town against him, or at least neutral, after your show at his mine, his options are more limited."

The crowd started milling around. Sam said loudly, "Somebody clean up the mess, will you?"

At first it looked as if nobody would follow Sam's request. Finally some of the crowd picked up Parrish's body to carry it away.

At the hotel, Jordan had stepped inside, followed by Strep and Caphorn.

CHAPTER NINETEEN

Nelson Jordan's face was grim as he faced his men in his office.

"I've had enough," Jordan said. "I've had it up to my neck, and I won't stand it anymore!"

The others in the room looked down at Jordan. Strep's bruised face had turned a splotchy black and blue. His hands were still steady, however, and he had a look in his eyes that Jordan could not read. Grant, his other key man, had so far managed to avoid getting hurt in the various confrontations with Hart, Matt, and Sam. He was still eager to help. Phil Caphorn looked bored with the whole thing.

"Talk's cheap," Caphorn said. "So far, all I've seen is that they've beat the crap out of you. So what are you going to do in return?"

Jordan gestured at Strep. "Now's the time to blow the dam. I want all of Hart's operations destroyed. I want him ruined. I want him dead. I want all of his men dead. I'm out of patience."

"You still think it's a good idea?" Strep asked.

Jordan glared at him. "I think you're getting mighty big for your britches," he said.

"Maybe. Maybe not. I agreed to work for you, not be your slave. I've given you your money's worth. I think getting myself killed wasn't part of the agreement."

"What do you mean?"

"For awhile, you had things going your way. Hart was a thorn in your side, but you had plenty of claims in your name and a mine started. You had plenty of people who would fight for you. Now it's not quite that simple. After the show that Sam and Hart gave at the mine, they've got a lot of support. Even from your workers. If shooting starts, they'll sit out — if you're lucky. Hell, I have half a mind to ride on myself."

"So I was right. You are a traitor. You're siding with my enemy."

"I'm still on your payroll. I just think you need to be warned this is not going to be a picnic."

"A picnic? Who's talking about a picnic?"

Jordan turned to the door, where Malinda was smiling sweetly. Her dress was dirty and her hair had worked loose. But she was smiling happily.

"Nobody invited you," Jordan growled. "You're a traitor, too. Joining up with the no-account drifter, Bodine."

"That's not fair," Malinda said. "I just wanted to let you know that if you want me to sing, tonight, I will . . ."

Jordan crossed the room before Malinda could finish her sentence. His hand made a quick movement and slapped the side of Malinda's face. The sound filled the room.

"You'll do what I tell you," Jordan said. "I said you don't belong here. Go back to your room. I'll take care of you later."

Malinda glared at Jordan, but turned on her heels and left, closing the door after her.

Malinda was hurt and she was angry. Though she had some problems with Jordan in the past, it was as if the slap had opened her eyes to other parts of him. They were parts she hadn't wanted to see before.

As she left the room, she shut the door, but left it open a crack. She quietly put her ear close to the crack to listen to the talk.

"There was no calling for that," Strep said.

"You just shut up. You're always been too uppity. I don't want any more argument."

Caphorn was smiling, though he didn't say a word.

"Here's the plan. We blow up the dam tonight. The water will rush through the streets and into Hart's land. That should cause plenty of destruction, but I want more than that, now. During the confusion, I want as many of Hart's men as possible to be picked off."

"Aren't you forgetting something?"

"You mean Bodine and Two-Wolves?"

"Of course. They're not going to just be sitting around twiddling their thumbs. And they're hell on wheels."

"That's what Caphorn is here for. He'll take care of those two."

"No problem," Caphorn said.

"By the end of tonight, they'll all be dead," Jordan concluded. "That'll clear the way for me to grab up Hart's claims and work this area like a real businessman."

Malinda pulled her head back from the door. She had been so wrong about Jordan! She still felt some loyalty to him, but she had to draw the line at so many innocent lives being lost.

She hesitated for a second. She had been with Jordan for a long time. It didn't feel right to go against him. Then again, he had never struck her before. She had never seen him so cold and ruthless.

Inside the room, movement started taking

place, and somebody started for the door.

Malinda had to make her decision quickly.

She hurried out the back door to try and find Matt.

Jordan turned to Strep.

"Can you go along with this plan? Or are you going to fight me on it?"

"I had doubts. But I'll finish this job for you."

"Good. Go on out and get the explosives ready." He handed a slip of paper to Strep. "My mining engineer drew up a diagram for me, showing potential weak spots. He thought I was looking into a safety project. Actually, you put explosive at those points, and the whole dam is guaranteed to give way."

Strep took the paper and left the room.

Jordan took out a cigar and lit it. After several minutes, with the cigar well-lit and smoking nicely, Jordan looked at the remaining two men.

"Well?" he asked.

"Strep's not a traitor," Grant said. "Maybe some of his decisions aren't to your liking, but he's not going to betray you."

"What's your thoughts, Caphorn?"

"Can't trust him. Whether he opposes you openly or not, he has his doubts. He's going

235

to drag his feet. He's going to make mistakes. I think you should get rid of him."

"Do it."

"It'll mean more money."

"Fine. Just do it. As soon as he sets the explosives. Make it look like he died in the explosion. I doubt if anybody will ever investigate this, but no use taking chances. We don't want to get sloppy."

Jordan turned to Grant.

"How many men remain loyal to me?"

"I don't know. Maybe a half dozen. Maybe a dozen. In the cover of darkness, it'll be enough."

"Then get to it. Make sure they're ready when the dam gives way."

Darkness was falling. Malinda wasn't exactly sure where Matt and Sam would be at this hour, but she had a guess. She knew that Hart and his men often met after hours at a little saloon owned by a man named Clancy. He was the one that Matt said made the wine that they had drunk on their picnic. It was only a little while before, though it seemed like days.

Malinda wished she had time to get cleaned up and change. But there was not enough time. She didn't know when the dam was going to blow, and she didn't want to take any chances.

When she got to Clancy's saloon, she hesitated again. She still had time to turn back. If she entered through the front door, then somebody would see her and report back to Jordan. It was now or never.

She stepped through the door.

Matt and Sam were seated at a table with Hart, Shannahan, and a few other men. Most of the men were drinking beer.

Matt was the first to see her.

"Malinda! What are you doing here?"

"I've got something important to tell you."

Hart said, "If it's personal, we can leave . . ."

"No. It's nothing like that. Jordan plans to kill you."

"That's not news," Sam said. "We've been waiting for him to make his play."

"Not just you, Sam, and Matt. But Hart. And as many of his men as he can shoot."

"Might be easier said than done," Sam said. "He hasn't done such a hot job, so far."

"No, you don't understand. He plans to blow the dam."

Matt stood up, took her hands in his. "Slow down," he said. "What exactly does Jordan plan to do?"

"He's going to blow the dam."

"And what will that accomplish?"

"I can answer that," Hart said. "The way the dam's built, water is diverted from this area, making digging operations possible for Jordan and for myself. But Jordan is better capitalized. He thinks he can rebuild while I'd be ruined."

"Would you?"

"I don't know. It'd be a severe setback. What's worse is the men it could hurt or kill. There's lots of people camping in the path of the flood. And my men who are working in the area could be killed."

"So that explains why he was moving his men to higher ground," Sam said. "I should have thought of that!"

"You're still not used to the white man's devious ways," Matt said.

"There's more truth to that than I care to admit," Sam answered.

Matt asked Malinda, "When do they plan to blow up the dam?"

"I don't know. I overheard the talk. I didn't hear everything that was said. I think they're going to do it tonight. They also plan to have some sharpshooters stationed around town to pick off as many of Hart's men as possible in the confusion. Caphorn is to get Matt and Sam."

"I'm going to the dam," Matt said. "Sam,

would you and Hart do what you can to get as many to safety as possible?"

"You got it."

Malinda had not yet let go of Matt's hands. She said, "Matt? I have a favor to ask you."

"All you need to do is ask."

"Try to take it easy on Jordan. I know it looks pretty bad for him. And I know he deserves to be punished. I'm not sure he deserves to be killed. I know it's stupid, but he has been good to me in the past. And I would hate to be the one who caused him to be killed."

"Don't worry, Malinda," Matt said. "I won't kill him in cold blood. Nor will Sam. You have my word on that."

"Thank you."

"Now, I want you to get back to the hotel. I want you someplace relatively safe when the shooting starts. This is one time you won't be able to help. No matter what happens, please stay in your room. I don't want your singing career cut short by a stray bullet."

Matt watched Malinda walk down the street through the open saloon door.

"No figuring women, is there?" Sam asked.

"I never have found a way."

"Here's a woman who may be risking her life by warning us of Jordan's plan. Yet, her final request to you is not to be too hard on Jordan. How can she have it both ways?"

"Ours is not to reason why, it's just to be confused as hell," Matt said.

"So true!"

Hart asked, "You know where the dam is?"

"I've seen it on some of my rides. Anything special I should know about it?"

"Not really. It's just a lot of earth and logs. It's pretty sturdy, but it wouldn't take much of a jolt for it to come crashing down."

"You all try and warn everybody. Watch out for Jordan's men taking potshots at you. I'll try and join you all when I can. If I can."

CHAPTER TWENTY

It was night, but the moon and stars were out, casting plenty of light for Strep to see to his work. He wondered if this time he had stayed with the job too long. This was not his kind of work. He probably should have said his piece and moved on. Let Caphorn and Jordan do what they wanted, and leave him out of it. But he had come this far, so he would stick it out.

Strep walked along the top of the makeshift dam, looked down into the deep water on one side, the relative dryness on the other side. The stream that was dammed up was barely a river, though now that its natural flow was diverted, it looked bigger than it was. And there was enough water that it would wreak havoc on the town once it was freed.

The dam had never been intended to be permanent in the first place. As Strep looked it over, he wondered how it had even lasted this long. It didn't look solid enough to hold five minutes. The gunfighter walked back and forth, looking for the potential weak spots that had been shown to him.

"Oh, to hell with it," Strep growled. "Who cares what some educated fool thinks. One spot's as good as another."

He paused on the other side, where some timber had been used to reinforce the makeshift structure. He inserted some explosive, and then a little more for good measure. He walked several paces down, and did the same in another section. He repeated this several times until he had crossed the entire length of the dam.

Strep remembered something about needing to blow the structure somewhere toward the middle. He got down to his belly, looked more closely at the side of the structure away from the water. It was not really dry, and in a few places a trickle of water seemed to seep through. On the other side, he heard the dark water splash in response to the slight wind that had picked up.

"Hell, do they expect me to climb this thing like a damned monkey?" Strep muttered. "They're lucky I'm out here at all. I should have told Jordan off and skipped town when those blasted blood brothers first hit town."

He reached down as far as he could, carelessly stuck in some explosive and let out some fuse.

"There, that's good enough," Strep said.

Satisfied with his work, the gunfighter moved back to the side nearest the town. He had almost made it to solid ground when the voice called out in the night.

"Stop right there, Strep. We know all about your plan. Drop everything and I won't shoot."

Strep yelled out, "Damn you, Bodine!"

The town of Jordanville seemed almost deserted. Even the saloons seemed quieter than usual.

"I figure most people in this town will stay clear of the shooting," Sam said. "The ones that are still in town. By now I suppose most everybody's scurrying for higher ground."

"I wish Jordan would call this craziness off," Hart said. "This feud's gone on long enough."

"He won't," Sam said grimly. "Like many men who've had a taste of money and power, he's not going to give it up. It's not just the money anymore. Now it's a matter of not being beat by you."

"You're right. I plan to stay here and build something. I want the earth to give its riches, sure, but I want to leave something behind, as well. Jordan would never give me any peace. Maybe it's just as well."

"If he hasn't caught on yet that his plan isn't working too well, he'll find out soon enough. With your men situated near the hotel and other areas near the hotel, we should be fairly well protected. Jordan probably has his men in place already, as well."

"I don't particularly like this place," Hart said, gesturing to the barn where Sam had decided to position him. "It's too far from the action."

"Neither one of us knows that. You're a steady hand with a gun, I think, and you can handle yourself in a close-up fight. You'll be needed here."

"I owe you a lot. I'll do as you suggest."

"Good man. I'm going to check on some of your other men. This promises to be a long night."

Matt knew exactly where the dam was. He rode quickly to it, but stopped his horse some distance away and made the rest of the way on foot. Already, the old streambed outside of the main area of town was starting to grow up, giving him plenty of cover. He wasn't sure which direction the water would flow, if he couldn't stop Strep in time, so he made sure his horse was tied on higher ground. And Matt tried to stay on higher ground as he approached the dam.

From this distance, the dam was not a pretty sight. It was mainly a long, rough shadow against the dark night. The moon and stars cast enough light to illuminate the top and edges of the earthen structure. It looked to Matt as if the dam wasn't too steady to start with and that a heavy wind could blow it over.

Matt moved as quietly as ever, staying in the shadows. He had no firm plan, only to try and stop Strep if he could.

Matt finally got in close enough that he could make out details of the dam. Movement caught his eye. It was Strep, belly-down on the dam, leaning over with his explosives. He was not quite within firing range. Matt moved in a little closer, positioning himself for a clear shot, if need be. He yelled out to Strep, who dropped to the ground again. He was temporarily invisible.

Matt took a shot, just to see if he could get a reaction out of Strep. No shots were returned.

Matt moved in a little closer when he saw the match flare up. He shot, but the bullet hit a tree between him and Strep.

"You can't get away with this," Matt said.

"Damn you, Bodine," Strep called back. "This is it for me. I'm gone."

Another shot sliced through the night. It was from neither Matt's nor Strep's guns.

Caphorn knew he probably should not have taken this additional job without first pocketing the money, but he was already tired of this poor excuse for a town. He wanted to get his work done and move out. If getting rid of Strep would get the job done faster, then that's what he would do.

Caphorn generally tried to at least provide the illusion of a fair fight when he killed somebody. It was good for his reputation. Sometimes, however, he was not quite so nice about it. This was one of those times.

He had waited until the fuse was lit, so that the dam would blow. Now, Strep's job was done and he was expendable. Caphorn again sited down the barrel of his rifle, aimed at Strep.

Caphorn fired again and again, each time bringing the bullets that much closer to their intended target.

He had figured that Matt would figure that somebody was helping him corner Strep, but the blood brother for some reason had stopped his shooting. Strep had heard some of the stories being told in town about Matt and Sam. If they were to be beieved, both of them were half-crazy. There was no telling what Bodine was planning now.

Strep leaped for safety, giving Caphorn his best shot yet, even if it was at a moving target. Caphorn fired another quick shot. This one was a solid hit.

As Strep fell to the ground, Caphorn considered going after Matt. Then the dam exploded, and Caphorn decided instead to return to town. The dam was crumbling, and if he guessed Matt's location correctly, he would be caught in the edges of the unleashed waters.

If the water didn't kill him, then he and Caphorn would meet in town.

Caphorn figured either way Matt Bodine would die that night.

Strep, on his belly, was inching away from the lit fuse. He was not surprised to hear Matt's voice or his gun.

The shot from the third person did surprise him.

The gunfighter would have generally taken the time to determine where his assailant was hiding and return some shots. With the lit fuse burning away, he didn't have that luxury this time.

He scurried backwards faster and faster.

A bullet hit just inches from his head. Strep knew it wasn't Matt shooting at him. It was from the wrong angle. Could it be Two-Wolves, or somebody else?

The fuse was getting near its charge. Strep stood, dived from the embankment into the brush below.

The lead slug hit him in the back as he dived through the air. The heavy metal tore through his skin, muscle and bone, exiting out the other side in a blur of blood.

He landed awkwardly. His leg was broken where he had hit the ground. Not that it made any difference. He could feel the life flowing out of the jagged wound in his body.

His eyes had gone sightless before the dam exploded.

Matt was puzzled. Who else had come to the dam looking for Strep? Matt knew it wasn't Sam, who was organizing forces in town. Maybe one of Hart's men? That didn't seem likely.

Whoever it was seemed to be out for blood. He fired shot after shot at Strep, who was trying to get away from the dam.

Matt paused. Should he also go after Strep? Or should he investigate the third person, now doing the shooting?

Strep suddenly came to an open area. He stood, tried to dive for safer cover in the brush, but it was too late. The slug hit the gunfighter solidly in the body, tearing a large hole in him as it exited. He fell awkwardly to the ground and lay still.

Matt knew the other man was dead.

But it was too late to stop the dam from blowing. Too much of the fuse had already burned away.

Matt stood to make a run for his horse when he felt the explosion before he heard it. The force of the explosion hit him like a gust of hot air. The roar followed a split second behind.

Matt turned to look. The explosives had not been set very well, and most of the dam remained intact. Several large chunks had been blasted away, leaving the top and sides uneven. The damage had weakened the overall structure, however, and already a steady stream of water was pouring over the top, eroding away the base of the structure on the other side.

In other parts of the dam, water was starting to stream through in a muddy mess. The top part of the dam almost seemed to weave back and forth under the force of the water.

Suddenly a massive chunk of earth split off and fell to the ground. Water gushed through the opening. The stream weakened the structure even more and several more sections dissolved into the water.

This had all taken only seconds, though to Matt it seemed like an eternity. He hurried even faster up the hill to his horse, to get back to town hopefully before the water hit.

Things didn't quite work out that way.

With a sound like a loud crack, the rest of the earthen dam gave way, unleashing the full fury of the water that had been trapped behind it. With a roar, it washed away what was left of the dam and took with it uprooted trees.

Matt, in spite of his precautions, couldn't avoid the onrushing water. He had no choice but to try and ride it out. He took a deep breath just before the water hit, and tried to relax and go with the torrential stream. The water hit him with an impact that took him off his feet and almost knocked the breath out of him.

Somehow he managed to rise to the top of the stream, where he gulped in another mouth full of air. He was being pelted on all sides by fallen limbs and roots. He was rushing down the old streambed at an amazing speed, though the new growth was slowing it down some. He reached out, grabbed a tree trunk and held on for dear life.

Jordan was in his office when he heard the explosion. His men had been stationed around town. They were supposed to wait until the water hit the town, forcing Hart's men into the streets, before they started firing. Even so, the brief explosion seemed to serve as a signal of some sort, and the gunfire started even before the waters hit.

That was unusual. Who had started the shooting?

He looked out the window, and was even more surprised. Several riders were rushing down the street carrying lit torches. It took Jordan a moment to realize that they weren't his men, and that they intended to torch the hotel — with him still in it!

In a moment Jordan realized that word of his plan had leaked out, and somebody had made plans for a counterattack.

Jordan hadn't planned to actually participate in the fight, and he had no weapon available.

Even if he had, the riders were coming too fast to stop them.

CHAPTER
TWENTY-ONE

Sam hadn't included torching the hotel in his plans. And had anybody asked his advice, he would have told them not to do it, since Jordan would have men stationed around the building.

Too bad the two riders with the torches hadn't asked his advice.

The two were riding fast toward the hotel, their torches held high, when the first shots were fired. The rider on the left slumped over his horse and fell to the street. His torch fell beside him and flickered in the dirt.

Sam noted where the shots had come from, and returned the fire. He heard a groan, indicating he must have hit flesh, whether he killed the other man or not.

The second rider continued on, and had a little more luck than the first rider. But it was only a little luck. He managed to toss the torch to the top of the building before he was brought down in a hail of bullets. His body was nearly torn to pieces as he fell.

Up and down the street, shots were being exchanged. Sam moved quietly down the street, staying in the shadows. He came upon two men standing by one of the buildings. They spotted him almost at the same time Sam saw them. Their guns belched flame. Sam hit the ground, heard the bullets whistle over his head. He shot upwards. One bullet barely grazed the groin of one of his attackers, making him yelp in surprise and pain. He dropped his gun and started running down the street.

Several more shots were taken at him, but they somehow missed him. He didn't bother to shoot back. He just ran faster, until he disappeared from sight.

The second man was a little more difficult. He managed to move to one side just as Sam's second shot was fired. That bullet harmlessly hit the building wall. The attacker got off several more shots at Sam, who continued to roll out of the line of fire. The bullets kicked up puffs of dust behind him as he moved.

Sam stopped behind a water trough and fired. His aim was mainly from instinct, but it was true. The lead hit his attacker in the stomach, doubling him over in pain. Sam fired again, this time bringing his attacker to the ground.

Sam did not have time to savor his victory. Somebody at his back was already shooting.

"I've got you covered!" a voice called out. "Get to safety!"

Sam looked around the water trough to see Shannahan running down the street, firing into the building where the last shots at Sam had come from.

Sam jumped up and dived into an open doorway.

Down the street, the torch had taken hold. Flames started to lighten the sky from on top of the hotel.

Sam wondered grimly if Jordan's plan would work against him, and if his men would be picked off as they fled the hotel.

Jordan breathed a little easier when the two riders with torches were killed, even though the second rider managed to toss his torch to the roof. That was not good. All of his men were positioned just outside the hotel. There would be no way to put the fire out.

For the first time, Jordan considered the possibility that things would not turn out as he had envisioned when he first came to this little mining town. First Hart, and then Bodine and Two-Wolves, had proven surprisingly tough.

He looked around his office, coming up with a plan. It might be just as well to get away for awhile to regroup. He walked over to a gun cabinet, unlocked it. In it were several rifles and shotguns of various makes and styles. He reached for one of the guns, then stopped. He was not good with guns. He had used them primarily for rare hunting trips outside of town, not for fighting other men. If he brought one with him, it would be an open invitation to shoot at him first. On the other hand, he might get into a situation where he needed a gun. He compromised by taking a small-caliber handgun that could be easily concealed.

Jordan then looked over the rest of his office to determine what he should take with him if he had to leave quickly — as it looked like he might. He would need his papers, of course. And some cash. Fortunately, much of his money had been safely stashed in a California bank, where it would be relatively safe. He would still come out of this alright.

He heard a ceiling cave in elsewhere in the hotel. The sound was almost drowned out by a roaring from outside the window. He stepped over to the window, careful not to make himself an inviting target.

A huge wall of water was rushing down the street and through the town. In seconds, it would hit the hotel.

Matt almost drowned in the onrushing water. If he hadn't been in such good physical shape, and had learned to swim so well at an early age, he might have died. As it was, he still had his hands full.

The tree trunk he had grabbed was old and gnarly, with some of the roots still attached from where they had been ripped out of the ground. Matt had grabbed one of the limbs as it rushed by him. He continued to be hit with other pieces of roots and trees, though by now he was almost numb and barely felt them.

The tree itself also moved wildly in the current, making it tough for Matt to keep his hold.

Matt slowly pulled his way up the limbs to the main body of the fallen tree. He reached out, grabbed hold of the rough trunk and hugged it close. This gave him somewhat better protection. It was still difficult to hold onto, but he managed to get his face above the water and keep it above the water.

The whole series of incidents had taken

only seconds, though it seemed like hours to Matt. Now, the water was rushing toward the center of town.

Matt could see only a little of the area immediately surrounding him. He couldn't be aware of the damage that was occurring because of the water.

He shook his head to keep water out of his eyes, and looked for a chance to abandon his ride and rejoin Sam and the others in town.

Grant saw Shannahan warn Sam about his attackers, but the miner managed to slip back into hiding before Grant could shoot. He took a few shots at Sam, who was now also retreating to safety. Grant missed, though it gave him some satisfaction to almost get the better of Sam Two-Wolves.

Not too far away, the hotel roof was in flames. It would be only a matter of minutes before the fire spread.

Already, several bodies littered the street. Some were Jordan's men. A few were Hart's. Matt had not yet been seen. That worried Grant somewhat. He was dangerous enough in plain sight. Who knew what might happen if he could sneak up on a person?

Grant headed in the direction that Shannahan had gone.

A face popped out from behind a building. Grant wasted no time. His slug hit the unwary miner in the face, killing him before he had any chance to shoot.

Grant continued down the street. He stepped onto a rain barrel and then onto the roof of a building.

He couldn't have timed it any better, for it was then he heard the roar and saw the solid wall of water rushing toward the town.

It hit with a tremendous impact. It took down all of the tents that had been outside of town and carried them along. Part of the water hit the ruined entrance to Jordan's mine, lifting the rocks like sand and washing them away.

Then the water hit the hotel. When the rushing water hit the fire, just now starting to shoot its flames into the sky, the sound was like the contents of a giant washtub being poured on a huge campfire. Steam rose into the air as the water extinguished most of the flames.

As the water hit the hotel, already weakened by fire, it also carried the front porch and much of the building along with it as well. The water seemed to gouge up some of the rough street as it went, making the water muddy as well as filled with trash.

Grant had little time to watch the destruction. A bullet whizzed past him and a second hit near his feet. He glanced over to see Shannahan on another roof, a few buildings down. Shannahan was shooting a rifle, though the roof he was on was at a slant, making it difficult for him to aim.

Grant jumped to the next building, firing at the Irishman. Shannahan shot back, though neither man was getting very close to their targets.

As if he realized his vulnerable position, Shannahan started to move carefully toward the edge of the roof. Grant shot again, this time placing the shot near Shannahan's head. The Irishman jerked his head back, and almost lost his balance.

Grant used this opening. He fired twice more, this time hitting Shannahan in the arm and leg. He dropped his rifle and fell.

Grant fired again, though he didn't know if he hit Shannahan again or not. The Irishman had disappeared into the water.

Hart had it fairly quiet. He had faced and killed several of Jordan's men — most of them apparently trying to get away from town any way they could.

Apparently Jordan was going to lose this battle, in spite of his best efforts.

Hart had climbed into the hayloft of the

barn where he had been placed to get a better view of the fight. It was then that he heard the roar of the rushing waters. The water from the blasted dam was rolling down the street and through the town, carrying with it bodies, trees, and pieces of buildings. Much of the fighting had apparently gone to the rooftops for that reason. He heard gunshots from several buildings away.

To his horror, he looked down and saw the lifeless body of Shannahan, his friend and employee, being carried downstream. He wanted to reach out, but now there was nothing he could do.

Below him, the water had entered the building, filling it to the depths of several feet. Then it just as quickly subsided. By now, the initial rush of the water had lost its force. With the pressure behind the dam unleashed, nature would quickly restore the stream to its normal, relatively slow and shallow movement. It would find its new course, possibly through what was left of the town, possibly outside of it.

Compared to the roar of a few minutes earlier, the town was now relatively quiet. Hart climbed down from the loft. His boots made sucking sounds as he walked through the muck in the bottom of the building and into the street.

To his surprise, all of the town was not covered in mud and muck. In a few places, the dirt and rocks had been washed away, as if with a hydraulic hose. He walked slowly, trying to avoid the worst areas and also keeping an eye open for Jordan's men.

He hadn't gone more than a few dozen paces when he came upon an area that had been dug out by the flood. It was now filled with water. Even so, Hart's trained eyes caused him to stop in stunned amazement. He got down on his hands and knees to better examine the rock that had been exposed at the bottom of the hole.

Unless he was mistaken, he had found an ore that would yield great riches. Not in gold, but in silver.

Though Hart and Jordan had come close to finding the main vein, the real treasure had been under the town itself all along.

Hart paused to consider what this meant. The town was not incorporated. He had laid claim to large chunks of land, much of it even he didn't know the boundaries. It was possible that the ramshackle town had risen on his land. In any case, with this additional clue, he could direct his mining activities more profitably.

So the flood had provided some good,

after all.

But it was at the cost of a life of a friend, as well as many other men.

Hart was lost in his thoughts, which was a mistake that he should not have made. He knew better, but the vision of his friend's dead body floating past him still haunted him and Hart was not as careful as he might normally have been.

A shot fired at him from a few buildings away woke him up, though almost too late.

Grant was still on the roof as the rushing water started to slow. He watched for other signs of activity, but the town now seemed almost dead.

Then he spotted movement several buildings down. He looked closer, and couldn't believe his luck. It was Hart himself, stepping out into the open, making himself a target. It was an invitation Grant couldn't resist.

From that distance, it was more a matter of luck than accuracy. This time, luck was on Grant's side. The bullet hit Hart in the leg. He screamed and fell to the ground. He fired back and tried to crawl back to safety, though his leg was instantly numb and refused to work properly.

Grant climbed down from the building to

make his way toward Hart, to see if he could finish the job.

Matt was getting his second wind. He had gotten used to the movement of the tree on which he had hitched a ride and had managed to catch his breath. The water was also slowing down, making his ride a little easier.

He pulled himself up a little higher. He couldn't believe he had traveled so far, so fast. He was already in town, passing the Jordan Hotel.

Or what was left of the hotel. Part of it had been burned. Part of it had been washed away.

Matt wondered if Malinda had gotten away to safety.

His thoughts were interrupted by a loud crash, as his ride crashed into a building. He let go of the tree as it turned and drifted away with the water again. Matt treaded water for several minutes as the water level seemed to lower. He swam for the building, grabbed hold of the roof and climbed on top.

Almost before his eyes the water slowed and its level went down, leaving mud and muck in its place.

Matt climbed down to the street, saw he had landed at the building that housed

Clancy's saloon and restaurant. He pushed open the door, but the place was empty except for mud and destroyed furniture.

He looked down at his holster, was surprised to see that his gun was still in its place. He looked around the bar until he finally found a rag that was not too damp, and some bullets wrapped in an oil-cloth in a room in the back.

Matt leaned against the wrecked bar, started to clean his gun and insert fresh bullets.

He felt in his gut that while Sam, Hart, and the others had probably taken care of most of Jordan's men, the one called Caphorn was his alone to deal with.

CHAPTER
TWENTY-TWO

Phil Caphorn had sat out most of the battle. After he had shot Strep, he stayed on high ground, above the dam, until the worst of the flood was over. And, incidentally, the worst of the fighting had ended.

It wasn't Caphorn's fight. He had been hired to kill a few specific men. That he would do.

After the waters had calmed, he directed his horse back toward town.

The destruction had no impact on him. If anything, Caphorn decided that this would be the best thing for such a little hellhole. Wash it off the face of the earth. Caphorn chuckled at his own joke.

It was always possible that Matt Bodine and Sam Two-Wolves had been killed in the flood or the fight, though Caphorn doubted either one. Those two were survivors, and it would probably take more than that to kill them.

He dismounted near the edge of town and started to walk slowly, in case there were any stragglers still shooting.

Caphorn wasn't really looking for Matt or Sam. He knew that somehow, their paths would cross. He thought about going into the hotel for a drink, but when he noticed how damaged it was, he changed his mind. There would be plenty of time for drinks after he finished this job, and there wasn't any use in delaying it any longer.

It didn't make any difference which one he faced first, Matt or Sam. He would get them both. He was sure of it.

Grant knew he had hit Hart. He had seen Hart go down. He had heard the scream. If he could finish off Jordan's enemy, there would no doubt be a bonus in it for him.

Sam also knew that Grant had hit Hart, though he was not in a position to help him at the time. He had also found some higher ground while the floodwaters had raged through town, and he had not gotten to a more strategic location before Grant had shot Hart.

It was now surprisingly quiet. Though the fighting had been fierce for a few moments, it had not lasted very long. Perhaps the flood had cut it short. Sam suspected, however, that Jordan's few men had either been killed or had skipped town after the fighting started. They had not expected to be faced with well-armed men who knew how to fight and didn't mind fighting.

The town was a mess. It would take a lot of work to clean it up. Sam figured, however, that Hart could do the job, if anybody could. Hart seemed to be in this for the long haul, unlike Jordan.

Sam sneaked a peek from behind the wreckage of one of the buildings. Hart could not be seen. That probably meant that the miner was still capable of movement, and had gotten to safety. Grant was probably also nearby, looking for Hart.

Sam heard a slight movement behind him. He whirled around, but did not shoot. One of Jordan's men was standing with his hands in the air, holding his gun by its barrel.

"Hey, don't shoot! Don't shoot!"

"Why not?"

"I'm out of it. When I signed on with Jordan, I didn't expect this kind of fight. I'm done. I'm leaving. I don't want to get killed."

"Throw away that gun." The man did as he was told. The gun plopped in a puddle. "Now get. If I see you again, I'll kill you. Got it?"

"I'm gone. I'm tired of tangling with you."

The exchange took only a few seconds, but it distracted Sam's attention away from the street. When he turned back around, he saw Grant running toward the area where Hart had been shot. Grant was apparently unaware he had been seen.

"Hey, in the street! Stop right there!"

Grant, surprised, turned and raised his gun. Sam shot first, stopping Grant in mid-step. He stumbled, fell. His gun shot harmlessly into the air.

Sam shot again, and this time Grant lay still in the street.

Malinda had an uneasy feeling, and it wasn't due either to the shooting or to the fire in the hotel. The flames had eaten through part of her ceiling, but she figured she was still safer there than in the middle of the shooting.

She looked out her window as the flood hit. Though the water crashed through the downstairs doors and windows, taking much of the hotel with it, her room remained fairly intact.

So she was still relatively safe. Then why did she feel so uneasy?

Part of it was Nelson Jordan. She wondered if she had done the right thing by warning Matt and the others of his plan to destroy the dam. After all, she did owe Jordan *something* for helping her. But hadn't she paid him back in other ways during the time they had known each other?

She had acted impulsively with Matt. But she hadn't really betrayed Jordan. After all, even though Jordan had promised her many things, it wasn't like they were engaged or anything. And while she liked Matt very much, Malinda knew that she had no future with him. He had made no promises, while Jordan had. The question now was, what was Jordan going to do?

Somehow everything had changed over the past few days, and she no longer knew what to expect from anybody, including herself.

She looked around her room, grabbed one of her small bags and placed a small handgun in it. Strep had given it to her several months before, to help protect herself during her rides in the country. Malinda had never found it necessary to shoot it, or to even pull it out of its usual hiding place. Most of the time it remained in a drawer in her room.

She hoped she wouldn't need it today. She wasn't even sure she could shoot a man.

Not quite sure what she would find, or

how she would react, she opened the door to her room to find Jordan.

Matt moved cautiously through the town. There was no movement and hardly any sound. Puddles remained in the street, and the stench of sour mud filled the air. Matt had carefully cleaned and dried his gun and checked the action to make sure that it would work flawlessly when he needed it.

Matt, like Caphorn, knew that he and the gunfighter would face each other. It was now a matter of when their paths would cross, though both knew tonight would be the night.

And they both knew that only one would walk away.

Matt's boots were wet and muddy. He had to pause every few minutes to clean the mud off them. It was slow going, but he was in no hurry.

Caphorn was the first man to spot the other, though it would have done him no good had he tried to get the drop on Matt, who fell back against a building wall when he spotted the gunfighter.

Neither man had pulled their guns.

"So there you are," Caphorn said. "I was wondering where you were hiding out."

"You're a fine one to talk. You look like

you managed to avoid the flood and the fight."

"Yes. I was rather lucky. Luckier than some of the other poor fellows out there, I'd venture to say."

"I'd guess you were probably above the dam when it broke."

"That'd be a good guess."

"And you probably were also the third shooter, the one that killed Strep."

Caphorn shrugged.

"You're facing me now. Not a green kid. Not a man who was shot in ambush. Think you can fight a fair fight?"

Caphorn laughed. "There's nobody around to watch. Why would I want to fight fair?"

"If you have to ask, you'd never understand."

Caphorn laughed again.

"Let's get to it."

Caphorn moved to the center of the street. Matt did the same. He was calm, his eyes deadly serious. His hands were steady.

"Just for curiosity's sake, how much are you being paid to kill me and Sam?"

"It might amuse you to know that I've got $30,000 in gold for you two. It's not the most I've ever made at one time, but it's close."

"I'm surprised we're so valuable. And here we are, helping Hart for free."

"Fools come in all shapes and sizes," Caphorn said.

"Of course, we don't need the money. And even if we did, we wouldn't take it for killing a man. Not even a poor excuse for a man like you."

It was a waiting game, a kind of cat-and-mouse, to see which one would break first. Caphorn was a professional who had killed many men. But Matt had been raised among the Cheyenne, and had learned patience in many ways, especially during the hunt and in war. He had faced not just loaded guns, but many other dangers in his young life. He was not afraid, and he was patient.

It was finally Caphorn who broke first.

His hand went for his gun. The movement was a blur. His gun was drawn and fired in the twinkling of an eye.

Except that Matt was just a split-second faster, and a little more accurate.

Caphorn's bullet cut through Matt's wet shirt, grazing the side of his chest.

Matt's bullet also missed its exact mark, though it hit Caphorn in the thigh.

The gunfighter, though hurt, refused to go down. He shot again. Matt had dropped to one knee, and the bullet passed over his head. Matt acted as if he had all the time in the world. He carefully aimed the gun squarely at Caphorn's chest and softly squeezed the trigger.

The bullet hit the gunfighter, entering his heart.

Still, he didn't fall.

Matt squeezed off three more shots in a tight pattern. Blood started to spurt from Caphorn's chest. He fell backward into the street, his gun still in his hand.

Matt stood slowly and walked over to the body. Caphorn stared up at him with lifeless eyes.

"Thirty thousand dollars, eh? That's a lot of money for a man who'll never get to spend it."

Blood oozed from the chest wounds into the mud of the street.

Matt reloaded his gun, then headed for the hotel.

CHAPTER
TWENTY-THREE

This was not working out at all as Jordan had envisioned over a year before. At that time, when he was working as an attorney for Clarence Hart, it had seemed so simple to maneuver his way into taking over Hart's claims. He could get rich as a lawyer, but he could get rich faster with a profitable mining operation.

And it might have worked, if not for those troublemakers, Matt Bodine and Sam Two-Wolves. If they hadn't showed up, his high-pressure tactics would have worn Hart down and the miner would have signed over his rights.

Now, Jordan had nothing. Even his hotel was charred and falling apart.

He looked around at what was left of his office, threw a few more papers in his satchel, preparing for his escape. He was surprised that some of the more important deeds and papers had survived the flood and the fire. The expensive safe he had brought in from California had proven a good investment, after all.

Or maybe it was an omen?

It wasn't entirely true that he had nothing. He had managed to put away some of his earnings in a bank back in California. He still had claims to some of the land surrounding Hart's. He still had his legal background and friends in high places. This particular plan had failed, but there were always alternatives.

Many of his men were dead, but they were only hired guns. They meant nothing to him. He could always get new men.

It was now relatively quiet outside. Jordan left his office, a small revolver in his hand, and entered the saloon area. The sawdust was now ashes. The stage had fallen in on itself.

Jordan paused. The brief relationship with Malinda had been an unexpected bonus. She had made him some good money. She had been an interesting companion.

No matter.

He could always get another singer.

The problem now was how to get out of town without being stopped by Hart, Bodine, or Two-Wolves.

Jordan heard a faint sound behind him.

He whirled, but did not shoot when he saw Malinda's familiar outline in shadow against the wall.

"I see you're leaving," she said matter-of-factly. "Aren't you forgetting something?" She was holding a small cloth bag.

"You mean you? Forget it."

"You'd leave me here?"

"Hitch a ride with your cowboy friend. Bodine would be glad to help you get where ever you want to go."

"He's a good man. I just can't understand how you could just walk out on me when, believe it or not, I've been loyal to you."

"Loyal, up to what point? You went off with Bodine as easy as you please. And I suspect you warned him about the dam blowing. Leave you here? It's easy. Watch me."

Malinda pulled a gun from her bag. "I don't know what you think about me. I'm not sure I care anymore. But I know that Matt wouldn't walk out on me like you're doing. You just stay right where you are. Matt may or may not kill you. But I think it's only fair that you meet him, man-to-man."

Jordan didn't hesitate. In a second, he had crossed the floor and grabbed Malinda's gun hand. He squeezed and twisted, releasing the gun. He grabbed it as it fell from Malinda's hand, then hit the woman with its barrel. Malinda fell to the blackened floor.

"So long, Malinda. It's been fun."

The woman was dazed, but conscious, as Jordan started down the street.

It had all come down to this: Hart's group against Nelson Jordan. All of Jordan's other men were dead. Only the ringleader himself was still alive, and to be dealt with.

Matt moved cautiously down the soggy streets, even though his main concern, Phil Caphorn, had been removed from the picture. Sam and Hart had made sure Jordan's other men had been taken care of. The streets were quiet now, but Matt knew that one or two potential assassins could still be lurking in the shadows. There was no use taking unnecessary chances.

Matt knew many of the Cheyenne methods of stalking, and moved almost without sound through the town. As he walked, he also thought of Malinda. He wished she would have agreed to go with him and Sam, and let them protect her. He had to respect her loyalty to Jordan, no matter how misguided, though he was concerned for her. Even if Jordan tried to keep her safe, which

Matt doubted, he would not be in a good position to keep stray bullets from going her way. It was as much with her in mind as in finding Jordan that Matt made his way to the ruins of the Jordan Hotel.

The outer walls were gone. The interiors were gutted and burned, though patches of roof gave scattered protection from the night. The small part of the collapsed stage that could be seen through the broken walls looked sad and alone. Was it only a few days before that Matt had first ridden into town and caught his first glimpse of Malinda?

Matt moved quietly into the gutted building. The air was silent and damp. Jordan was nowhere to be seen.

Matt entered the room that had served as Jordan's office. In one corner, a small safe stood open. It was charred on the outside, but looked clean and smooth on the inside. Matt guessed that Jordan had been here recently to pick up some papers and flee the town. Such a move wouldn't surprise Matt.

He heard a slight moan from the saloon area. Matt hurried through the door to find Malinda on the floor. He kneeled beside her, took her hand.

"Are you alright?" he asked.

"Matt? You were right. I should have come

with you."

Matt helped the woman up, tried to wipe off some of the soot from her dress.

"Are you hurt?" Matt asked again.

"I'm tired. I want to go home."

"I'm going after Jordan. You stay here, away from any more shooting. You understand?"

Malinda nodded.

Matt continued down the street.

It had seemed like all-out war to Clarence Hart. It was a war he had been ill-prepared for. He was a miner, not a soldier. Though he had been ready to fight, he had no idea it would ever come to this.

The barn in which he had situated himself, like everything else in town, was damp and cold. The initial effects of the blown-up dam were relatively short-lived, even though it had caused much destruction. The longer-term effects were to leave a coating of mud over virtually every building and to fill the air with dampness and a smell of rot.

There was, of course, the unexpected benefit of helping to find the main vein. It was silver ore, not gold, but was rich enough to provide the fortune that Hart had worked toward for so long. It was ironic that the force of the water rushing from behind the dam had dug out enough of the soil to expose the ore. In a strange way, Jordan had done Hart a favor.

If he managed to live through this night.

Hart glanced down at his leg. The constant dampness was of more immediate concern for him, since infection could easily invade the wound. It had finally stopped bleeding, though it had soaked through his pants and rough bandage made from an old shirt. Hart could barely put any weight on his leg, which now throbbed with pain. He wasn't sure if the bullet had hit bone or not.

The position that Sam and Matt had asked him to man had been a good one. From his place in the barn, Hart could see the street leading to the rear of the former Jordan Hotel. In the street were the bodies of three men who had tried to sneak in on Hart's forces. Hart didn't really know them, except by name; they were some of the guns that Jordan had hired and brought in. Now the street was quiet. It had been long minutes since Hart had seen any person, friend or foe, on the street. Maybe it was now time to get out and explore a little. His help might be needed elsewhere.

Hart stood slowly. His head felt faint as pain shot through his leg. He looked around for something to use as a crutch, but found nothing. He gritted his teeth and used one hand on the wall to pull himself up. He kept the rifle in his other hand.

Progress was slow. He pulled himself along the rough wall to the door. No shots greeted his arrival, so he continued into the street.

The mud was squishy, and made his progress even slower. He made his way over to one of the bodies in the street. The dead man continued to clutch his revolver. Hart bent down to take a closer look. The gun was still clean and the man had a belt full of cartridges. Hart started to remove the gun. He figured he could handle it better with one hand.

Though the street was deserted, Hart felt strangely vulnerable. It seemed like it was taking forever to free the gun and then additional bullets. Hart almost dropped some of the bullets as he transferred them to his pockets.

His thoughts seemed to come in waves. He suddenly realized he made a wide-open target. What was he thinking? That wasn't a mistake that Matt or Sam would have made. It wasn't a mistake that he should have made.

How many bullets would he need? How many of Jordan's men were left?

He had no way of knowing.

He decided he had better not make himself such an inviting target. But his legs would not move fast enough. He headed for the corner of a building, but progress was agonizingly slow. When he finally reached the building, Hart was breathing heavily and he felt very tired. He looked down at his leg. It was bleeding again.

Hart wondered, *Where were Sam and Matt? And where was Jordan?* Hart had wanted to face Jordan man-to-man, to at least partially avenge the destruction that he had caused. Was Jordan now alive or dead? Were Hart's friends alive or dead?

Hart heard footsteps squishing in the mud from down the street. He lifted his gun, in case it was an enemy instead of a friend, but the gun seemed very heavy.

Suddenly, Jordan's face came into focus.

"So, Hart, it finally comes to this? Just you and me?" Jordan kicked the gun out of Hart's hand. It landed in the soft mud. "You know, Hart, it all would have been mine already, except for your friends. And that frustrates me." Jordan glanced down at the bright red blood on Hart's pants. "So that's it?" Jordan continued. "It's your leg?"

Jordan kicked. His boot tip struck Hart's leg solidly. The pain felt like fire, and it took everything Hart had to keep from screaming.

"Yes, I see you're in pain," Jordan said. "Well, here, let me give you a little something to remember me by."

Jordan stepped forward, bringing his foot down hard on Hart's wound. It started bleeding even harder, and Hart could almost feel the crunch of bone under skin. Jordan moved his heel in hard little circles, as if he were putting out a cigarette.

Hart tried to hit back, but the pain was now too great. Finally, the pain eased into unconsciousness.

Jordan finally removed his foot when Hart slumped to the ground. Jordan briefly considered killing Hart, but then decided his claims would be tied up too long in the courts. And what if he had any heirs? It would probably be better to take on a powerless, defeated Hart in the courts than some anonymous court-appointed probate attorneys.

Jordan pulled out a cigar, lit it, puffed happily, and then continued down the street. He figured he would find a saddled horse in one of the buildings.

Sam knew Hart did not really like the position where he had been placed. The miner preferred to have a more active role, but realized he could do more good where he was at. Judging by the bodies in the street, Hart had done his job well.

Sam figured Matt would check out the remains of the hotel and see if he could find Malinda. Sam decided to keep his eyes open on the main avenues out of town. The streets were now so quiet, however, that he expected few more problems.

Even so, Sam kept a careful eye on the streets as he walked. He entered the barn where Hart had been positioned. He called out softly, "Hart? It's Sam!"

The only response was silence.

Sam moved in carefully. He noted the fresh bloodstain on the floor and along the wall where Hart had been standing. That meant that Hart had been hit, though he was still alive. At least alive enough to move to a new location.

Sam followed the trail of blood into the street. When he saw Hart's body slumped in the street, he didn't hesitate. He covered the ground in only a few long strides and kneeled beside the miner. Hart groaned slightly. So he was alive, though his face was twisted in pain.

With a practiced eye, Sam checked out the wound. He decided that even though Hart had lost blood, he would probably live.

"Hold on a little longer," Sam said, picking the other man up easily. "I'll get you someplace safe."

"Jordan . . ." Hart muttered. "He did this . . . to my . . . leg."

"We'll see what we can do for him," Sam said. He positioned Hart in some clean straw in the barn. He checked the wound to make sure it hadn't started bleeding again. It wasn't the best of circumstances, but it would do for now.

Sam stood, checked and reloaded his guns, then stepped outside to find Jordan for the final time.

CHAPTER TWENTY-FOUR

Matt continued to move cautiously through town, even though he felt now that he had little left to fear. Jordanville, never much of a town to start with, now seemed to be almost empty. Matt decided this was one place he would be glad to put behind him.

Matt had a pretty good idea what Jordan's next move would be. He was a city-bred attorney, wily in the ways of the legal world, but now he was in unfamiliar territory. He would not know how to cover his trail or to find a backtrail out of town. He would probably find the nearest horse and take the most direct way out. So Matt cut across various back alleys that he had become familiar with during his short stay to cut off the escape route.

He came to a rock outcropping that he had remembered, climbed up the rocks to position himself and wait for Jordan.

The night now seemed strangely quiet. All

mining operations had temporarily ceased. The normal sounds of night — insects, night birds, and frogs — could again be heard. As he waited, Matt decided that in spite of the problems, he did not regret his stay here. He was not the marrying kind, and might never be. Even so, he was glad he had met Malinda. He wondered what would happen to her now.

Matt was seated comfortably, and could wait for hours, if necessary. It was only a matter of minutes, however, before he heard movement. It was a slight sound that perhaps would have been missed by other men.

"Hey, Sam," Matt called out softly. "Looks like great minds think alike."

"Does that leave you out?" Sam answered, in an equally soft voice.

"Come on up, you old dog."

Sam scurried up the rock to take his place beside Matt.

"I must be slipping," Sam said. "I didn't think anybody could have detected my movement."

"Most men wouldn't," Matt admitted. "But I know your movements. I could probably sense your presence blindfolded in a herd of stampeding buffalo."

"Let's hope you never have *that* splendid opportunity!" Then, more seriously, he said,

"I found Hart. He's in bad shape. He's a tough bird, though, and I think he'll live. Jordan did a number on him before I found him."

"A man shows his true colors when his back's to the wall," Matt said. "He's had a busy night. He mauled Malinda before he fled."

"Did he think he could really get by with his scheme?"

Matt shrugged. "Why not? Others have gotten by with a lot more. If not for our presence, he might have succeeded."

"He might still have a chance."

"What do you mean?"

"If he escapes, he would be free to hatch some other plot. Though he's committed every kind of crime imaginable, there's not enough law out here to deal any justice. He'd be free to make another land grab. If not here, then elsewhere."

"Then let's not let that happen."

"I'm moving to the other side of the road. I want to make sure he doesn't sneak by us."

"He won't."

It was more difficult to find a decent horse in the ruins of Jordanville than Nelson Jordan had expected. He had to look through several barns and outbuildings in town before he finally found a saddled horse. Jordan didn't care who had owned the horse before; it was his, now. He was quickly up in the saddle and headed out of town.

Matt and Sam were looking for him. Jordan felt it instinctively. On the other hand, he had a good start on them and was confident that he would escape cleanly. He probably should have spent less time in his "farewells" to Malinda and Hart, as much as he had enjoyed it. There was nothing he could do about it now, however.

The horse he had found was nothing special. It had a slightly awkward gait as it stepped through the muddy streets, jarring him slightly with each movement. He was glad he wouldn't need the horse for long. He'd trade horses at the next town he came across. With luck, he'd soon be back in California.

Though he had failed in his plan to monopolize all the mineral rights in this part of the country, he was still relatively satisfied. In spite of the obstacles in his path, he had made a great deal of money and he had learned some lessons. For one thing, he wouldn't get sidetracked with a woman. While Malinda had made him some money, she had also been a distraction. He also planned to hit his opponents harder, both legally and with a better class of gunfighters. He was still fairly young, and had done alright for a first-time project of this type. So what if most of his men had been killed? It was just a cost of doing business. Besides, it gave him some great stories to relate to his brothers and cousins back in California.

Things remained quiet. It was too quiet. He was now almost outside of town, and had not been stopped. It was almost too easy.

He kicked his horse to proceed faster. The ride became bumpier, but it was getting him out of town faster.

It was just a few moments later that he heard the voice call out slightly in front of him and to the right: "Stop right there, Jordan. We've got you covered."

Malinda knew that Matt had her best interests in mind when he told her to stay put, to keep her out of danger. In the past, the woman might have done as she was told. Before she came West, she dared too little on her own. Now, she realized she could do anything she wanted to do.

So after Matt left to go after Jordan, Malinda followed in his footsteps.

Before she left, she walked over to a locked cabinet near what had been Jordan's desk. It was charred, but still relatively intact. The fire had weakened the lock. The woman easily broke it open to reveal the guns inside. She was basically untrained in firearms, knew she would have little chance at being accurate. So she selected a small-bore shotgun that Jordan had sometimes used in hunting trips.

Malinda had no firm plan in mind. She just knew that Jordan had violated her in ways she never would have understood before she came West. Now she also knew that if she wanted vengeance, she would have to seek it herself.

She also had the vague thought that she might be able to help Matt in some way.

Malinda had watched Jordan load the gun many times before. She found some shells in the case that had somehow survived the fire, inserted them into the gun.

Satisfied that she could carry the gun with little difficulty, Malinda stepped into the street to try and catch up with Matt.

Matt was the first to spot Jordan. He waited for Jordan to move well into firing range before he called out. In response, Jordan stopped his horse and raised his hands.

"I'm stopped," Jordan said. "No need to shoot!"

Matt slid down the rock to the road, all the while holding his gun on Jordan. On the other side of the road, Sam stepped into view. Both approached Jordan cautiously.

"Get off the horse," Matt said. "Keep your hands in plain sight."

Jordan did as he was told. He was a little stiff from the uncomfortable ride.

"Going on a trip?" Sam said.

"Actually, I am," Jordan answered. "My business here is done. I'm going home."

"As easy as that?"

"The way I look at it, boys, I'm not cut out to be a fighter. I'm still hurting from the bruises your friend, Hart, gave me. And I'm certainly not a gunfighter. Do you expect me to fight my way out of this situation?"

"You're going to let us take you without a fight?" Sam asked.

"Excuse me, may I smoke?" Jordan slowly reached into his pocket and pulled out a cigar. He lit it slowly, methodically. Only when it was puffing nicely did he continue. "Take me where?" he said. "To a court? Back to town, where I might still have a few people who are loyal to me? What are your choices? That is, if I don't fight, and I don't intend to. If I fight, I would just give you boys a rationale to kill me."

"An interesting philosophical dilemma," Sam said.

"Yeah, you would find it interesting," Matt said. "I think all those hours in the university softened some of those brain cells."

"As you might have figured by now, I don't think a whole lot of you two," Jordan said. "I think that there's probably not a lot you would do if given the chance. But in your own way, you have a sense of honor. I don't think you would kill an unarmed man in cold blood, no matter what grievances you might have against him."

"He uses as many big words as you do, Sam," Matt said. "Since you speak the language, what do you think?"

"I'm tempted to shoot him and be done with it," Sam answered, truthfully. "But he is right. I have never killed any man in cold blood for any reason. I like to think it makes us better men than scum like Jordan. If the grievances were against us personally, I might could justify such an action."

"So we can't shoot him," Matt said.

Jordan smiled, put the cigar in his mouth, puffed contentedly.

The sudden roar of a shotgun blast filled

the night air and Jordan's smile died on his face.

The shot had hit him squarely in the chest. Jordan lived long enough to look in surprise at the blood that suddenly soaked his clothes. He then pitched forward, landing facedown in the mud. The cigar fell a short distance away, still smoldering.

Malinda stepped out in the open from a hundred feet down the road.

"Maybe you boys couldn't shoot," the woman said. "But I could."

Sam stepped forward, nudged Jordan's body with the toe of his boot. "I spotted you down the road," Sam said to Malinda. "I wondered if you had what it takes."

Malinda let her gun fall to the ground.

"Would you have actually let him walk if I hadn't shot him?" Malinda asked.

"An interesting philosophical question," Sam said. "It doesn't make much difference now. It's over. Let's go get Hart."

Matt had already put his arm around the woman and was leading her back to town.

CHAPTER
TWENTY-FIVE

Matt Bodine and Sam Two-Wolves saddled their horses. Sam was going through his motions quickly, Matt a little more slowly. Both were more than ready to leave this poor excuse for a town, but Matt wanted to have a few more words with the former Malinda Melody, now just Malinda Smith.

Hart, limping slightly on his bandaged leg, came out of the small saloon to say his goodbye. Malinda followed him, wearing a plain cotton dress and carrying a small satchel. She remained just inside the doorway while Hart walked up to the blood brothers.

"I sure wish you boys would change your mind and stay longer," Hart said. "I really feel there's a future here. Now that I finally struck the mother lode, I plan to start major operations soon. I'd let you boys in on the ground floor."

Matt and Sam looked around at what

remained of the town. The Jordan Hotel was now nothing but cold ashes. Much of the equipment had been destroyed, and what remained was quickly rusting.

In the town cemetery were too many new graves. Jordan's body was being shipped back to California. Most of the other dead men had been buried in the town cemetery. Nobody would miss the gunfighters like Jack Parrish and Strep Menson. The good men, including William McFey Shannahan, would be missed. Sam wondered how many more good men would die trying to reap the mineral riches from these mountains, and if modern men would ever learn to do as the Indian did and live in harmony with the Earth.

"As we explained the first day we met you, we're ranchers, not miners," Sam said.

Hart, favoring his bad leg, shook his head slightly.

"Ranchers you may be, but you're also two of the best fighting men I've run across. You're good with your fists and your guns. And you're developing a reputation as fighters. That might bring you attention you don't need or want."

"We're just living our lives. We're not looking for trouble. But we don't run from it, either."

"Even so, you're making new enemies all the time. For all you know, Jordan may have kin tougher than him. If they care enough to pay for his body being shipped back home, they may care enough to come looking for revenge. Some of Jordan's men are tough hombres. They're scattered now, but who knows when your paths might cross again?"

"We'll take it one day at a time. I don't intend to let what *might* happen spoil my enjoyment of life. As far as I'm concerned, the best is yet to come." Sam glanced over at Matt, who was still toying with his saddle. Sam asked, "You about ready to ride?"

"Just about." He glanced up at the woman in the doorway. "Give me a few minutes with Malinda."

"Sure, brother. Take all the time you need."

Matt cinched his saddle, patted the horse's smooth hide, and walked up to the woman. She smiled, but did not put down her satchel. Their voices were low, just out of hearing distance for Sam and Hart.

"I'm glad you dropped in on me like you did," Malinda said. "It doesn't seem possible that a few days ago we had never even met."

Matt smiled back. "I would have liked to

have gotten to know you better. But the situation wasn't exactly working in our favor. I'll remember your kiss. And I'll remember your singing." He gestured at her satchel and said, "You're heading out, too?"

"I decided to go home, back East. I came West to have an adventure. That I did. Too much so. Never in my wildest dreams could I have imagined singing in the middle of a wilderness. Or almost getting myself killed, and watching so many others get killed. I've seen enough. I'm going home. Hart is giving me a ride to where I can catch a train home."

"What do you plan to do when you get home?"

"I don't know. My dad wants me to get married. But I just can't see myself settling down yet. I feel like I have so much left to see and do . . ."

"You should stick with your singing."

"You are very flattering, Matt."

"No. I mean it. You are good."

"But the competition back East . . ."

"Hogwash. You have the talent and can do whatever you put your mind to. Don't give up. Not now." He paused, then awkwardly continued, "I'm not near ready to settle down yet, either. But maybe someday, if I find my way back East, and you might consider coming West, I might come calling."

"You do that, Mr. Matthew Bodine." She reached up, kissed Matt on the cheek. "You just drop in on me anytime."

Matt turned and walked back to his horse.

Sam for most of the conversation between Matt and Malinda had politely kept his head turned away. But he glanced around in time to see the woman kissing Matt, and couldn't resist giving him a little kidding, to lift his spirits if nothing else.

Sam smirked and said to Matt, "If I could bottle whatever attraction you have for women, I would never have to work another day of my life."

"I've never seen you work that much to start with."

"I've worked you over enough times, and I could do it again, if you don't shut that confounded trap of yours."

"You're just jealous because the women you meet are not just ugly, they can't even sing!"

But the insults were in jest, and the blood brothers were smiling as they talked.

"You boys are sure cut from a different kind of cloth," Hart said.

Sam and Matt waved their final goodbye and started their ride out of town.

For long minutes, the two young men were quiet, lost in their own thoughts. They rounded a curve, and came upon the sign to one side of the rutted road in which the original name of "Silver Creek" had been crossed out and "Jordanville" painted in. That name had now also been crossed out, and "Silver Creek" repainted in the remaining space. The two men stopped their horses, and looked back at the town.

"What do you think, Matt?" Sam asked. "Is Clarence Hart fooling himself? Or do you think he'll find his fortune?"

"Hart's a good man. The West needs more men like him. He'll do alright. I can't say the same for the town. I imagine it'll be like so many other mining towns. Booming today on the promise of gold or silver. Gone tomorrow when the gold runs out, or never reaches its promise. It seems a shame that so many men have died here fighting over riches that might never be."

"Malinda will also be fine," Sam said. His voice was more serious than usual, though the familiar twinkle was in his eyes. "In fact, I'd say she came out of this better than either one of us."

"How do you figure?"

"Look, she's free to go her own way, and here I am . . . stuck with you . . ."

Before Matt could respond, Sam laughed loudly and spurred his horse down the road. Matt paused for only a second, then also laughed and joined his horse in the race.

Already, the air was becoming clearer as the two blood brothers left the mining town behind them, headed for another adventure elsewhere in the West.

ABOUT THE AUTHOR

William W. Johnstone is the *USA Today* bestselling author of over 130 books, including the popular *Ashes, Mountain Man,* and *Last Gunfighter* series.

The employees of Thorndike Press hope you have enjoyed this Large Print book. All our Thorndike and Wheeler Large Print titles are designed for easy reading, and all our books are made to last. Other Thorndike Press Large Print books are available at your library, through selected bookstores, or directly from us.

For information about titles, please call:
(800) 223-1244

or visit our Web site at:
www.gale.com/thorndike
www.gale.com/wheeler

To share your comments, please write:
Publisher
Thorndike Press
295 Kennedy Memorial Drive
Waterville, ME 04901